Chris Crowther
Timecruiser

Illustrated by
Sarah Rogers

TALEWEAVER

First published 2018
Taleweaver
PO Box 1239
Norwich
NR12 8XF

Cover art and illustrations by Sarah Rogers
Cover design and formatting www.jdsmith-design.com

Printed in Great Britain by Clays Ltd, St Ives plc

ISBN: 9781999811105

To Thomas, Millie and Amy

Another three young voyagers
who love the Broads

AUTHOR NOTE

Dear Reader

Opposite is a sketch map of the Norfolk Broads showing all the places you'll encounter in the story. If you want, you can use it to follow the children on this trip of a lifetime.

Good luck.

Chris

The Norfolk Broads

Sketched by
Sue Crowther

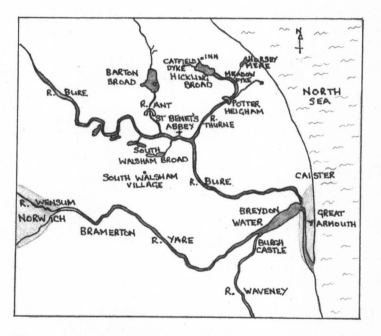

This is how the Broads look now, but remember that back in ancient times, Great Yarmouth and the land it's built on didn't even exist, and some of the settlements then were just islands.

Chapter One

"You have reached your destination."

'Thank goodness for that.' Slowing the car slightly, Mrs Watson reached across and switched off the sat-nav. 'I thought those winding Norfolk lanes were going on forever.'

Beside her, Mr Watson heaved a sigh of relief, turned and smiled at the three youngsters in the back. 'Right, everyone, all we have to do now is find the boatyard. Drive slowly, love. It must be along here somewhere.'

'HERO RAFT. Is that it, Dad? It looks a bit run down.' Squashed in the back between her twin brother Max and their best friend and classmate Faru, Jenny had spotted a tatty-looking sign with stick-on letters, hanging askew from a rotting gatepost.

Her father gave a nervous cough. 'Oh dear, it is. It's supposed to say HERON CRAFT. Two of the letters must've fallen off.'

Warily, Mrs Watson turned into the entrance and slowed to a crawl as they bounced along an increasingly potholed track.

'What a tip,' muttered Jenny, as the car lurched between the skeletal remains of rotting boats and piles of rusting discarded machinery. For the past two years, the family had spent wonderful holidays afloat on the Norfolk Broads, but Heron Craft was very unlike the smart boatyard they'd hired from before.

'Yeah, more like a scrapyard,' agreed Max, briefly glancing up from the game he was playing on his iPad.

'Oh come on you two, lighten up.' Mr Watson was sensing his family's disappointment. 'A boat's a boat, and lucky for us Heron Craft had a cancellation.'

'I bet they get lots of those,' mumbled Max, as he zapped another alien.

'Well, there's the office,' pointed out Mrs Watson, turning the car towards a shed-like building with the word RECEPTION barely legible above its half-open door. 'Not long now and we'll be afloat.' She glanced over her shoulder. '*You're* still glad you came, aren't you, Faru?'

'Oh yes, Mrs Watson. I can't wait.' On his first holiday with the family, Faru was trying to sound enthusiastic. 'Just a little stiff and hungry, that's all.'

'I expect we all are after our early start.' Mrs Watson stopped in front of the office and switched off the engine. 'It's been a long drive from Rugby, but as soon as we're checked in, we'll stock up with food from the shop and get you lot fed.'

'What shop?' Jenny was feeling increasingly dismayed as she recalled the miles of featureless countryside they'd just travelled through. 'I haven't seen any *sign* of a shop and I'll go mad if I have to stay in this car much longer. We've been cramped in the back here for hours.'

'Three point four, actually,' said Faru, glancing down

at his watch and mentally juggling some figures, 'to come 128 miles, which means we've travelled at an average speed of 37.6 miles per hour.'

Jenny rolled her eyes and gave him a playful nudge. 'Trust you to work that out, brainbox.'

'You're just as bad, Jen, with your head always buried in history books,' chipped in Max, eyes still fixed on his screen.

'Well at least I don't spend all my time on *that* thing,' snapped back his sister.

'OK, stop arguing you two,' ordered Mr Watson, climbing stiffly out of the car. 'I'll go and check in. The sooner we're off, the better.'

As his father disappeared into the office, Max glanced out at the rickety buildings. 'I just hope the cruiser's alright.'

'I'm sure it will be,' replied Mrs Watson with more optimism than conviction. 'It's not your dad's fault we couldn't hire one from the usual yard. That mess-up with his holiday dates meant they were fully booked. But you'll all feel better once we get going.'

'*If* we get going,' sighed Jenny, seeing her father coming back out of the office with a far-from happy expression, together with a rather overweight man in overalls and a two-day growth of beard stubble.

'This is Mr Dursley,' introduced Mr Watson, through the open car window. 'He owns the yard.'

'Mornin' all,' greeted Mr Dursley with forced jollity, touching the peak of an old sailor's cap stained with several layers of grease, oil and paint. 'Sorry, but there'll be a bit of a delay gettin' you away. Last week's hirers managed to put a hole in yer boat, so we're fixin' another ready for you that's almost as good. Take a little while yet though.'

Mrs Watson glanced anxiously at her watch and sighed. 'How long?'

''bout an hour, Ma'am.'

'OK, I suppose we can use that time to go and buy some supplies. How far away is the nearest shop?'

Mr Dursley nodded towards the gate. 'There's a village store a couple a mile on from where you turned off. Get all yer want there.'

'Two miles!' exclaimed Jenny. 'We've had enough of being in the car, Mum.' She was looking longingly beyond the yard to where the river flowed gently by. 'Can't we just hang around here until you get back?'

'What do you think, Mr Dursley? Do you mind us leaving the children here?'

'Fine by me as long as they don't go botherin' my workers.' The yard owner pointed between the sheds. 'Plenty of boats there for them to look round.'

'But would you be willing to keep an eye on them?'

'Not if I'm gettin' your cruiser sorted, I won't, but the prof's over there workin' on 'is boat.'

'Prof?'

'Professor Hazlelade. Bit of a funny old boy full of weird ideas, but friendly enough. I'll give the young'uns their lifejackets and they'll come to no 'arm.'

'Right then, kids, grab your rucksacks and off you go. Just make sure you behave yourselves and do as you're told. We won't be long.'

Jenny watched with mixed feelings as her parents drove back up the track and out of sight. She had hoped they would be on the river by now, digging in to a hearty fry-up, but at least this would give them time for a snoop around the boatyard by themselves. She picked up her rucksack. 'Right, let's get our lifejackets and then go and explore.'

'Why do we always have to do what *you* want to do?' Max was still engrossed in his game. 'Couldn't we just find somewhere to sit and . . .'

'No Max! We need to stretch our legs.'

'And there are sure to be lots of interesting boats to look at,' said Faru. 'So come on and turn that game off.'

After getting their lifejackets, Jenny led them between the leaning lapboard sheds and piles of nautical jumble, to finally emerge at a small marina where about twenty boats lay moored with their sterns to the quay-heading. By now a slight breeze was dappling the water and stirring the branches of a magnificent willow tree that cast its cooling canopy over the nearside corner. The river flowed alongside and, beyond that, stretching to the very horizon, endless marshes, their flatness and desolation broken only by the decaying stumps of windpumps that had once drained these wetlands. Jenny took a deep breath of invigorating Norfolk air and sighed. 'Isn't this just great?'

'Not if this lot's anything to go by,' grumbled Max, briefly looking up from his game to scan the marina, where most of the boats were wooden, with peeling paint and flaking varnish. Two had sunk completely with only their floating fenders still above water.

Jenny noticed Faru had lagged behind and was looking at an old sailing cruiser. She sauntered back to join him. 'Something special about this one?'

'Just that it's a sailing boat.' There was a little

glimmer in his eye. 'Bet you didn't know, Jen, but I'm pretty good at sailing.'

'How come? You haven't even got a boat.'

'No, but my uncle in Bangladesh has a small trader which he sails in the Ganges Delta, and he taught me.'

'Wow, Faru, when was that?'

'Two years ago. Mum and Dad hadn't been back there since I'd been born and thought it was time I met my relatives and saw where they grew up.'

'And did you enjoy it?'

'I had a brilliant time. It was a lot different from life here, though. My cousins didn't have half the things I did, but they were allowed to play out more and had much more fun making up their own games.'

'Not like my brother then,' said Jenny, glancing ahead to where Max had stopped. He was staring angrily at a blank screen. 'Uh oh, what's his problem now? I suppose we'd better catch him up and find out.'

Her brother was cursing. 'I was about to get onto my highest level and now the damn battery's given up and needs recharging.'

'Well, thank goodness for that,' sighed Jenny with relief. 'Welcome back to the real world. Perhaps now we'll get some sense out of you.'

But Max ignored his sister's remark and was grumpily stuffing the iPad into his rucksack, when something caught his eye. 'Hey, look at that.' He was pointing across the marina to where a rather strange boat lay moored beside the uneven quay. 'I bet that's the prof's boat. Mr Dursley said he was a bit weird.'

It certainly was the oddest-looking boat any of them had ever seen, its purple steel hull pointed at both ends, a short mast with a sail of sorts furled against it and a cabin that seemed to be the green body of an old Land Rover.

'Look, someone's moving about inside,' said Jenny. 'Let's go and see if you're right.' She strode ahead, leading the boys around the moorings until they were alongside the strange boat. She read the lettering crudely painted on the bow. '*Eldridge Echo*. That's an odd name.'

Faru scratched his head. '"Eldridge",' he repeated. 'You know, I'm sure I've read about another boat with that name.'

But Faru's musings were interrupted by Max, who had just spotted some heavy cabling running around the outside of the boat's steel hull. 'Look at this, guys. I wonder what that's for?'

'Ah, you might well ask, young man,' came a well-spoken voice from the cabin doorway. They all looked up to see a tall, thin, stooping man who looked about as old as the twins' grandfather. His mop of unruly white hair was straggling and unkempt, but the face beneath was both intelligent and kindly. 'Are you interested in my boat?'

It was Faru who answered. 'It *is* very . . . well . . . different.'

'It's certainly that.' The man smiled and nodded over his shoulder. 'Want to have a look on board?'

'Err, Mum and Dad'll be back soon . . .' hesitated Jenny, slightly wary of accepting an invitation from someone they'd only just met, though this old man was obviously trusted by Mr Dursley, they were almost fourteen now and there *were* three of them, '. . . but we'd love to.' As she clambered up onto the side-deck, she asked, 'Are you the professor?'

'I am indeed, and welcome aboard *Eldridge Echo*.'

By this time Faru had joined her, followed swiftly by Max who, tactless as ever, blurted out, 'What a heap. It looks like it was thrown together in some scrapyard.'

'Max!' Jenny cringed at her brother's rudeness.

But the professor didn't seem to have taken offence and just smiled. 'In a way, she was. The hull was an old ship's lifeboat that I bought at a breaker's yard. I'd just stopped driving and was about to sell my much-loved Land Rover when I realised it would do as the wheelhouse and cabin. Here, have a look.' He led them through what used to be the Land Rover's passenger door and down into the cabin. 'This is what I call "the nerve centre".'

Wide-eyed, all three children tried to take in the mixture of old and new, where a traditional wooden ship's steering wheel and solid brass fittings shared the old vehicle's cabin with three data-filled computer screens, flashing lights, rows of instruments and other numerical displays. Rather than a boat, it all seemed more like the cockpit of some hybrid spaceship. From below came the rumble of a powerful diesel engine. 'Is that from the Land Rover too?' asked Faru.

'Yes, but at the moment, I've only got it set up to generate electricity, not to drive the boat.' He nodded towards the banks of electronic gadgetry. 'To run all this takes a lot of power.'

'So, what exactly are you doing with all this . . . stuff?' asked Jenny.

'Oh, just an experiment I've been working on for many years.'

'To do what?'

'Primarily, to place a field of electricity around the hull.'

'So, *that's* what all those cables outside are for,' said Max.

'Well-spotted young man and, yes, they are indeed. You see, a problem with boats and ships is that all sorts of marine life like to attach themselves to their hulls. Anti-fouling paint helps, but it costs a lot of money. My theory is that a few volts of electricity will work even better.'

Jenny looked concerned. 'Surely that will kill the fish, won't it?'

'Er . . . no . . . just keep them away.'

'But, Professor, this is a stack of equipment just to keep the hull clean and . . .' However, Faru's query was suddenly interrupted mid-sentence by a sound like the chiming of Big Ben.

'Ah ha . . . that's my phone,' explained a seemingly relieved professor, searching for the elusive instrument before finally finding it beneath a pile of paperwork. 'Hello . . . Hazlelade . . . yes . . . oh, I see, that must be my new optical drive . . . right, I'll come straight over.' He turned to his young guests. 'Sorry I can't stop to answer any more of your questions, but a courier has just arrived at the office with a part I badly need. You'll have to excuse me while I go and collect it.'

'Oh right, I suppose we'd better leave you to it then,' said Jenny reluctantly, sad not to hear more about this peculiar boat from its eccentric owner.

Professor Hazlelade sensed her disappointment and smiled. 'I shan't be long actually, and I *would* like to show you the rest of the boat. If you like, you can just wait here until I get back.'

'That would be ace,' enthused Max, himself now totally absorbed by the computer displays. 'Are you sure you don't mind?'

'Not at all, as long as you *promise* not to touch anything.'

'We promise.'

'Right then, I'll be back in a tick.'

*   *   *

As the old scientist disappeared towards the office, the three examined the humming electronic activity around them.

'This is amazing,' gasped Jenny, overawed by it all.

'All this just to keep a few weeds off the hull,' said Max. 'What a waste of money.'

Surprisingly, Faru agreed. 'I think you're right.'

'How do you mean?' Jenny wasn't used to her brother being right about anything.

'I mean I just don't believe all this is to keep the hull clean. These electronics must've cost a bomb - more than a hundred *years'* worth of anti-foul paint.'

'Perhaps he's got bigger plans for the idea. If he proves it can work on this boat, it might work on big ships too.'

But Faru still shook his head. 'Yeah, maybe, but the power needed to do what he's talking about would use loads of energy.' His eyes narrowed slightly. 'I think it's all a cover-up for something far more involved than anti-fouling.'

'Hmm, you might be right,' agreed Jenny. 'And did you two think he looked relieved when his phone rang?'

'Yeah, probably because he didn't expect kids like us to ask awkward questions,' reckoned Max.

'Perhaps he's some sort of spy,' suggested Jenny, who loved reading thrillers as well as history books.

'If he was, he wouldn't have left us to nose around.'

'And none of this seems to be undercover stuff anyway.' Faru was examining some of the switches and dials.

'So, what do *you* think he's up to then?' asked Max, tapping one of the computer screens. 'Like all these weird numbers. What do *they* mean?'

'Stop it, Max! We promised not to touch anything.' Jenny was becoming anxious. It would be typical of her brother to do something stupid.

'She's right, Max. Keep your hands off.' Faru was looking at a smaller screen with four digits displayed. 'Well, this one's obviously showing the year.'

'But it must do something more than just *that*,' reasoned Jenny, unimpressed. 'Max, what on earth are you doing now?'

Bored with looking at figures, her brother had turned his attention to a large red lever set just to one side of the screen. 'Now, this is more like it. It must be the throttle. The old chap said the engine wasn't set up to drive the boat, but if you wanted it to go forwards, you'd just push it like this . . .'

'Leave it alone, Max!' warned Jenny. But it was too late. Even as Max moved the lever, there came an ear-piercing whine and a teeth-chattering vibration, while a blue mist seemed to envelope the whole boat.

'What's happening?' she screamed, covering her ears.

It was a question none of them could begin to answer before Faru darted to the lever and pulled it back to neutral. The whine stopped, the mist started to clear and the vibration ceased.

'You idiot, Max. You were told to leave things alone,' Jenny shouted, panic-stricken.

'I . . . I . . . didn't think it would *do* anything,' stammered her shaken brother. He glanced around the cabin. 'Anyway, it doesn't seem to have done any harm.'

'No thanks to you. I just hope the professor didn't see what happened.' She felt a little calmer and glanced outside to see if he was on his way back and, as she did so, all thoughts of being told off vanished.

The blue mist had almost completely cleared, but the scene it revealed was so unexpected, that Jenny's heart missed a beat. She rubbed her eyes and blinked hard, but when she looked out again, the vista had not changed. A feeling of dread welled up inside her as she stammered tremulously, 'The . . . the boatyard . . .' she pointed outside with a shaking finger, 'it's . . . it's gone!'

Chapter Two

Dashing to the cabin windows, Max and Faru were horrified to see Jenny was right. The old boatyard, with its dilapidated sheds and decaying quayside, had somehow been replaced by smart modern waterside houses set beside an extensive marina holding sleek new motor cruisers. Just behind the houses, a lofty wind-turbine turned with a rhythmic swish of its flashing blades.

'Wh . . .what's happened? Where are we?' cried Jenny, beside herself with foreboding.

'I don't kn . . . know.' An ashen-faced Max turned to his friend. 'All I did was push that lever and the boat seems to have moved.'

Faru was looking baffled. 'I . . . I don't understand, because we haven't moved. Look over there.' He was pointing towards the far corner of the marina where the spreading branches of a large tree brought shade to the two houses either side. 'I'm sure that's the willow tree we saw when we first arrived . . . so what's going on? Why's everything changed?' In desperation, he looked back at the instrument panel and suddenly the blood drained from his face. 'Max, it's not the boat that's moved, it's . . .' he tapped the digital number display that still winked to one side of the lever, '. . . it's this.'

'What?'

'The number.'

The twins both stared at the screen.

'It's gone forward ten years!' exclaimed Jenny. 'That can't be right. It would mean . . .'

'. . . we've travelled into the future,' gasped Faru, voicing the words Jenny was almost too scared to utter.

'Get real, you two,' scorned Max. 'Things like that only happen in science fiction films with whacky professors building time mach . . .' He stopped mid-word as the most terrifying thought hit him. 'Oh no! You're not saying that's what Professor Hazlelade's been secretly experimenting with?'

Faru nodded. 'I think so. He must've been dabbling in some anti-gravity experiment to achieve quantum tunnelling through space and time.'

'For goodness' sake, talk English, Faru,' pleaded a fraught Jenny. 'Are you saying that this boat is some sort of time machine?'

'What other explanation can there be?'

Jenny was almost beside herself. 'But, if you're right, we're stuck in a time ten years ahead of where we were.'

'No we're not!' exclaimed Max, colour returning to his face, 'because, if pushing that lever took us forward in time, all we have to do is pull it back and we'll return to our own time.'

'. . . and Mum and Dad,' added Jenny, with a sniffle and a watery smile.

Faru could only agree. 'It makes sense. Shall I try?'

'Oh please do,' begged Jenny, 'and quickly.'

'Right . . . here goes.' Faru firmly pulled the lever back, but this time there was no whine from below or outside mist. The only change in the boat's state was the quiet buzzing of an alarm and a flashing light on the instrument panel.

'What's the matter? Why isn't anything happening?'

'We mustn't panic,' said Faru, trying desperately hard to appear under control. He nodded to Max. 'What's it say by that flashing light?'

'LOW BATTERY.'

'Oh no!' Faru shook his head. 'I guess we've drained the batteries.'

Jenny glanced around her in desperation. 'But surely there's *something* you can do.'

'Don't worry, we'll get it sorted. First thing is to find out what state they're in.' Faru frantically scanned the instrument panel before spotting the bank of gauges. 'Here we are – BATTERIES – and these instrument needles have gone from a green arc to a yellow one.'

'Which means. . . ?'

'. . . they're low, but not completely flat. The good thing is, the engine's still running.'

'So, they're already charging back up?'

'Yes, helped by the solar panels on the roof.' Faru was studying the battery gauges. 'But slowly though. I reckon it'll be a while before we dare to try again.'

'By which time poor Mum and Dad'll be going crazy wondering where we've got to,' moaned Max.

'A pity you didn't think of that before you pushed the lever, you pea-brain,' scolded a furious Jenny. 'You *knew* the professor told us not to touch anything, but you had to show off, didn't you, and now look at the mess we're in.'

Faru silently agreed with Jenny, but could see Max was full of remorse, and bickering wasn't going to help the situation. 'Look, you two, what's done is done. Once the batteries are charged, we should be able to return to our year. Who knows . . . if your parents are a while shopping, we may still get back before they even notice we've gone.'

'Except the professor will be wondering what on earth has happened to his boat,' groaned Jenny.

'We'll worry about that once we're back.' Faru shrugged his shoulders. 'In the meantime, we've got at least an hour to kill before we can leave.'

'We could go ashore and look around,' suggested Max. 'After all, it's not every day we get to see into the future.'

Jenny looked apprehensive. 'Will it be safe?'

'I don't see why not, as long as we don't go far.' Faru was scanning the marina. 'There doesn't seem to be anyone about, so we should be OK.'

Pulling herself together, Jenny picked up her ruck-sack. 'Right, let's go then. I'll follow you two.'

*   *   *

Climbing down onto a well-maintained quay-heading, they cautiously made their way around the orderly marina. From the opposite side, Faru looked across the water to check *Eldridge Echo* wasn't attracting unwanted attention. All was fine, but seeing the cabling around the hull suddenly triggered his memory. He turned excitedly to the others. 'Guess what? I've just remembered where I read about a boat called *Eldridge*. It was in a book on scientific myths.'

'You mean the professor's boat?'

'No, the one in the book was a United States warship, the *USS Eldridge*, at their navy yard in Philadelphia, carrying out some sort of experiment to deal with magnetic mines.'

'I've heard of magnetic mines,' said Max. 'Don't they explode when a steel ship passes over them?'

'That's right, so the Americans fitted huge electric cables around the *Eldridge*'s hull, with the idea that a heavy current might neutralise its magnetic field.'

'Just like the professor's done with his boat.'

'Exactly, Max, except that things didn't quite work the way the Americans expected.'

'Why? What happened?'

'When they turned the power on, the whole ship disappeared.'

Jenny's mouth dropped open. 'What, you mean a whole big warship just . . . vanished?'

Faru nodded. 'That's what people watching said, and that the ship reappeared once the power was turned off.'

'But surely you don't think this is what's happened to us?'

'I know it sounds daft, but you have to admit there are similarities.' Faru put a comforting hand on Jenny's shoulder. 'Don't worry, Jen, at least the warship came back, and I'm sure, once the batteries have charged, we'll be able to go back too.'

'And then I'll be able to get my iPad up and running again,' chipped in Max. 'I'm desperate to get onto that next level.'

'I can't believe you just said that.' Jenny put her hands on her hips and glared at her brother. 'Here we are, stuck in another decade, not knowing what's going to happen next, and all you can think of is your blessed iPad. If it means that much to you, Max, I'm sure you'll be able to find a socket somewhere to plug the damn thing in.'

'It certainly shouldn't be a problem here.' Faru was indicating the towering wind turbine with its blades turning steadily above them. 'That'll be generating loads of power.'

'You're right, but what's going on with those wind-pumps?' asked Max, who had temporarily forgotten his iPad, and was staring out across the marshes on the other side of the river, where a scattering of white sails were turning in the freshening breeze. 'Surely they weren't working when we arrived at the boatyard with Mum and Dad.'

'No, they were all derelict,' agreed Jenny, equally puzzled. 'I don't understand. We're supposed to be in the future, but this is how the marshes must've looked a hundred years ago.'

'So, how come they've spent all that money restoring them now, when electric pumping stations have been doing their job for years?'

'Tourist attractions?' suggested Jenny.

But Faru shook his head. 'Hard to imagine, stuck out there in the marshes, but I just wonder if they're using all that free wind to generate electricity, by rebuilding the mills so their sails drive turbines instead of turning water-wheels?'

'It makes sense to me,' replied Jenny. She glanced towards the houses surrounding the marina where every roof was covered in solar panels. 'Maybe they have to rely on renewable energy for *all* their electricity now.'

'It would be good if they did,' approved Faru, setting off once more around the marina. 'Come on, let's not waste any more time. We've got loads to find out while we're here. To start with, have we really travelled ten years into the future?'

'Well, that's easy enough to check,' said Jenny. 'All we need is a newspaper.' But, though they searched, there were none to be found, not even in the large re-cycling bin beside a sun-cream dispenser. 'So, what do we do now?' she sighed, as they plonked themselves down on a grassy patch beside the water.

Casting his eyes along the river bank, Max spotted a young woman sitting at a small table in front of a narrow-decked garden, reading from the screen of a very modern-looking tablet. 'How about we go over and talk to her,' he suggested. 'She looks friendly enough – and I wouldn't mind a closer look at that bit of kit she's holding.'

Agreeing, they got to their feet and walked along a narrow footpath towards the waterside property. Once close enough to be heard, Max cleared his throat and gave his most charming smile. 'Hi.'

The young woman looked up, surprised. She was slim with long dark hair and dressed in denim shorts and a polo shirt that bore the logo, HERON BOAT

SALES. 'Oh, good morning to you.' Raising her sunglasses, to reveal striking brown eyes, she took just a second to examine the youngsters. 'Did you just come in that strange boat over there?'

'Yes we did.' Jenny was conscious that their arrival must have been something of a drama. 'I hope we didn't scare you.'

'Not at all. I love anything that's quirky, especially if it floats, and I haven't seen that old wreck for years. One minute the berth was empty and then, when I looked up, there it was. Have you come far?'

Jenny was almost tempted to say, "about ten years", but instead muttered vaguely about coming from somewhere downriver, before adding, 'We're just having a holiday here.'

'What, on your own?'

'No.' It was awkward, but Jenny decided a partial truth was probably best. 'The owner of the boat had to go and collect a part.'

'I see.' The young woman cocked her ear towards *Eldridge Echo*. 'I can hear its diesel engine running.'

The throaty rumble could be clearly heard in the otherwise quiet marina. 'Yes, that's right. We're just charging the batteries.'

'But doesn't the owner know about the by-law?'

Jenny bit her lip. 'What by-law?'

'The one that came out five years ago, banning all petrol and diesel engines on the Norfolk Broads. All motor boats have to be electric now.'

'Ah, but ours is an experimental boat,' explained Faru, thinking on his feet and earning a relieved look from Jenny.

'Well, if your owner's got an exemption, you'd better have his certificate ready.' The young woman nodded upriver. 'The ranger will be along in about an hour and you'll get a ticket if you're in violation.'

'Oh, we'll be gone by then,' promised Jenny, crossing her fingers behind her back and looking to Faru for reassurance.

Faru nodded. 'As long as the batteries have charged.'

The young woman gave a knowing smile. 'A pity you couldn't plug into one of our charging points. Since they restored all the old windpumps and converted them into wind-turbines, there are points even in the remotest parts of the Broads now.'

Faru looked smug as Max asked, 'So does the wind generate enough electricity to power all the boats?'

'Pretty much. That and solar power. Here, let me show you the change it's made to the environment.' The young woman tapped her screen and, turning it towards them, pointed to two images. 'You see, this was taken when we still had diesel and petrol engines polluting the air and water, and this one was taken earlier this year. You can see for yourselves the improvement in water quality and how little wash the boats are making.'

The change for the better was obvious to the youngsters, but it was the date beside the second picture that really grabbed their attention. 'So, is this definitely the year we're in now?' Faru asked.

'What an odd question. Of course it is.' Seeming a little puzzled, the young woman tapped the screen again to return to her original news page with its blazing headline.

'"SPACE TRAVEL HOLIDAY BOOKINGS

ROCKET"',' read Max over her shoulder. 'That looks interesting. Can I read it?'

'You can hear it if you want,' she said, giving the screen another tap to produce a well-modulated voice reading the day's news.

'That's so cool. It makes mine look really old.' Max pulled out his iPad from his rucksack and handed it across.

The young woman smiled. 'Good grief, that brings back memories. I had one of these when I was about your age.' She tried to switch it on, but before Max could explain that the battery was flat, there came a loud ping from her own. 'Oh, I forgot, the drone is delivering a spare part for one of my boats very soon.'

'A drone?'

'Yes, they're great for special deliveries . . . especially as they now let you know when they're five minutes from touchdown . . .' There came another more urgent pinging from her device, '. . . or *four* minutes it's telling me now.' She handed Max back his iPad. 'Sorry, but I've got to dash.'

'You said "your boats",' persisted Max, as she stood up. 'Do you have your own then?'

'Not really. I sell other people's.' Turning to leave, she fished in the top pocket of her shirt, brought out a card and handed it to Jenny. 'Here, give this to your skipper and tell him when he wants to replace that scrapheap, I can do him a good deal.'

Jenny read from the card. 'APRIL LANDERS – YACHT BROKER.'

'That's me . . . or at least for the next few weeks until I get married.'

'That's exciting. Is your boyfriend a yacht broker too?'

'No, he's an airline pilot.'

'How cool's that?'

'Yes, I can't wait for the big day.' She smiled. 'It's been great chatting to you. Enjoy the rest of your trip and watch out for the river ranger.'

They said their goodbyes and, as they hurried back to *Eldridge Echo*, Max looked over his shoulder. 'She was all right, she was.'

'Bit smitten were you, Max?' Jenny never missed the chance for a dig at her brother. 'Little old for you, isn't she?'

'Oh, shut up. I meant she was just nice, that's all.'

'Yes she was.'

They were soon back at *Eldridge Echo*. 'Let's see what shape the batteries are in now,' said Faru, going straight to the instrument panel, where he was relieved to see they were fully charged. With the ranger's visit imminent, he lifted the cover from the console to one side of the wheel and shut down the engine. All became silent with no more warning lights or buzzing alarms.

'Phew!' they all said in unison, and high-fived each other.

Faru went to the year lever. 'Right . . . here goes . . .' As he eased it back, there came a healthy whine followed by the now-welcome blue mist forming outside. 'Plenty of power this time and, look, the numbers on the year-gauge are moving back already.'

'Thank goodness for that.' As the vibration built up and the years started to click off, Jenny could feel some of her anxiety giving way to relief – that is until she saw the years were rolling back very fast. As their own approached, she yelled to Faru, 'Slow down, or we'll overshoot.'

'I'm trying, but the lever seems stuck!'

'What!' She turned to her brother. 'Quick, don't just stand there. Help him.'

Max sprang to add his own weight to the lever, before turning and giving his sister a despairing look. 'It's no good . . . it won't budge.'

*   *   *

With the whine and vibration increasing, to the youngsters' horror the year-gauge confirmed they were indeed accelerating into the past, whirring through the 1900s and into the 1800s at a faster and faster rate. 'For goodness' sake, push the lever forward again,' Jenny screamed. 'We're into the Nineteenth Century now and still going back in time.'

'We're trying, but nothing's happening,' came the terrified reply.

More whining, more vibration and, through the blue mist outside the cabin windows, clouds were scudding past below them. 'Faru . . . Max . . . I think we're flying.'

'. . . and backwards through the centuries as well,' Faru yelled back.

Petrified, Jenny could see for herself that they were plummeting ever-faster into the past - 1700 . . . 1600 . . . 1500 . . . 'My God . . .' she stood transfixed, dazed by the unreality of it all, '. . . we're going mediaeval!'

'Worse than that . . .' Faru paused only long enough

to use his sleeve to wipe a drop of sweat from the end of his nose, '. . . we've just entered another millennium.'

Indeed, the years had decreased into just three figures.

'Where's it going to end?' moaned Max in disbelief as he stepped back from the lever and put his head in his hands.

As if in answer, there came the buzz of a warning horn and the flash of an orange light which illuminated the instrument panel. 'Now what?' cried a distraught Jenny.

'Oh no, BATTERY LOW,' groaned Faru.

'You mean we've flattened them again?'

'Not quite . . .' He pointed to the battery gauges, '. . . but they *are* back down into the yellow arcs and we're already losing power.'

Sure enough, the drop in years was decreasing and outside the cabin windows, clouds flashed past as they descended, to see some islands, a large estuary and an expanse of sea sliding below. Not having any idea of where they were, but sure a crash was imminent, Jenny braced herself. By now the whine had decreased to a background hum and endless marshes were filling the cabin windows. And then the sound stopped completely and *Eldridge Echo* came to a gentle rest in what seemed like a waterlogged reedbed.

There was a stunned silence until Jenny whispered, 'Wherever are we?'

'And *when* are we?' added Max, weakly.

That last question was easily answered. The year gauge now stood at 279.

Jenny apprehensively looked out of the windows

at the acres of marshland around them and gave a cautious sigh of relief. 'At least it looks as if we're still somewhere on the Broads.'

'But that's a fat lot of good if we're now a thousand years into the past,' Max snapped back at her.

'Well over seventeen hundred years, actually,' corrected Faru.

'Oh screw your arithmetic. The fact is, we're now in the second half of the third century. What on earth does that mean?'

'It *means*,' answered a very scared, but ever-so-slightly enthralled Jenny, 'that we're back in Roman Britain.'

'Roman Britain!' wailed Max, immediately imagining the fierce-looking legions they'd learned about in school. 'Then let's just hope no-one saw us land.'

But Jenny wasn't listening to her brother. Instead her attention was fixed on the rhythmic clunk of oars getting ever closer.

Chapter Three

'What's that noise?' Max had heard it too.

'Sounds like rowing . . . and not far away.'

Eldridge Echo had come to rest in a narrow dyke, not much more than a wide ditch cutting through the reedbeds, but another boat nearby meant they must be close to open water.

Max scanned their surroundings anxiously and dropped his voice to a hushed whisper. 'It's getting closer, but I still can't see anything.'

'Or hear voices either,' murmured Faru, who had opened a side window to listen, 'so I'm guessing it must be just one person.'

Jenny hoped he was correct, but all they could do was sit tight and pray that, hidden by the reeds, they had not been seen and that the boat would pass them by.

But, far from getting quieter, the sound of blades dipping in water was getting louder. Seconds seemed like hours as they waited, hearts pounding, senses alert, until, agonisingly slowly, the curved bow of a wooden boat appeared around the reedbed. Then the rest of the boat glided into view, pointed at both ends, roughly but sturdily built, about four metres in length and being rowed by just a solitary girl of similar age to themselves.

Dressed in simple sackcloth, her long auburn hair matted and straggling as it fell over slender shoulders, she pulled tentatively at her oars up the narrow dyke before glancing behind and catching her first sight of *Eldridge Echo*. She stopped rowing, frozen into instant immobility, her mouth a silent O of disbelief as she stared with wide brown eyes at what had to be the strangest vessel she had ever seen.

'She looks even more scared of us than we are of her,' whispered Max, relieved it wasn't a boatload of Roman soldiers.

Faru nodded. 'No wonder. Our boat must look like some alien craft from outer space.'

'Except she'll never have heard of aliens *or* outer space.' Seeing that the terrified girl had grabbed her oars and was about to take flight, Jenny darted towards the cabin hatchway, pulled it open and called out, 'Hello there, don't go. We're lost. Can you help us, please?'

The girl shook her head and began rowing feverishly away.

'Ple...e...ase,' implored Jenny, tears starting to trickle down her cheeks.

Across the few metres of water, the stranger paused in her strokes. Perhaps it was a plea from a girl her own age that made her slowly back her oars and warily close the gap between the two boats. 'Who . . . who are you?' She spoke with a strange accent, but her voice, though edged with fear, was soft and clear.

'We're travellers from another village,' answered

Jenny, quickly realising the truth would be impossible to explain. She leant down, gave a friendly smile and offered her hand. 'I'm Jenny and this is my twin brother Max, and our friend, Faru.'

The girl pushed back a straggle of hair to reveal a face streaked with grime, but very striking nonetheless. 'I am Edith.' The small hand she offered in return was hard and calloused from work and rowing, and there was still suspicion in her voice. 'Are you Saxons?'

Jenny had to think very fast. 'No . . . err . . . Midlanders.'

Edith shook her head. 'Are they from over the sea?'

'No, but far from here.'

Max turned to his sister. 'So, who are the Saxons?'

'Raiders from across the North Sea,' explained Jenny from behind her hand, before turning back to the lone rower. 'No, we're friends.' Seeing the girl visibly relax, she pressed on, 'Where is *this* place, Edith?'

'Gariensis Ostium . . . the mouth of the Gariensis. It leads out to the sea. The forts guard its entrance.'

'Forts . . . what forts?'

'The new fort here of Gariannonum, and, on the other side of the great estuary, the older fort of Caister.'

'We know Caister,' said Jenny quietly to her brother and relieved some inkling of their position was starting to dawn. 'You remember, Max, it's right by Great Yarmouth, and I think what Edith is calling "Gariannonum" must be Burgh Castle.'

'You're joking! I remember us going round the Roman fort there on holiday last year and it was just a ruin. So, that means the estuary we saw just now must be Breydon Water, but I didn't see Great Yarmouth.'

'That's because it doesn't exist yet.' Jenny was recalling information she had read on that same holiday. 'A sandbank built up at the mouth of the estuary, and Yarmouth was built on that hundreds of years later.'

Faru was fascinated. 'So there's no land between these forts at Caister and Burgh Castle - just a huge estuary that opens out into the sea.' He turned to Edith. 'So, are there soldiers at these forts?'

'Oh yes.' She nodded in the direction of what must be downriver. 'At Gariannonum, there are hundreds of men and horses. What the Romans call "auxiliary cavalry".'

Max shuddered. 'We're right by a real working Roman fort. How scary's that?' He frowned at Faru. 'Why on earth haven't you got that engine running and the batteries charging? With all these Romans about, the sooner we're out of here the better.'

'Just calm down and use your head, Max, before getting all uppity,' retorted Faru. 'The noise of that engine will bring every Roman rushing from miles around to see what's causing it. Forget the engine . . . we'll just have to rely on the solar panels to do the job.'

'Which means we'll be here for ages.' Max turned and looked warily back to Edith. 'So, are you a Roman?'

'No, I am a Briton, though everyone in the empire is a Roman citizen. I live in a village very close to the fort and sometimes work there. I was out for an early row when I saw . . .' she tentatively tapped *Eldridge*'s steel hull, '. . . your strange boat. Is it bronze or iron?'

'Neither, but something like that,' answered Jenny, wondering how to explain Twenty First Century technology to someone living in the Third. Besides, the young girl seemed keen to leave and was already turning her boat around in readiness.

'Oh, don't go so soon, Edith,' begged Max. 'Please stay longer so we can get to know you better.'

She shook her head. 'Sadly, I cannot. It is an important day at the fort. Marcus Pomponius, the Count of the Saxon Shore, is inspecting the garrison, and there will be a great feast in his honour. I am to be one of the serving girls.'

'A feast, you say,' said Faru, his mouth watering. 'I bet there'll be loads of food to eat. What I'd give for a plateful of that.'

'Me too,' chorused the twins.

'I say, Edith, I know it's a big ask, but I don't suppose you'd be able to bring us some scraps when you finish work? We're all pretty hungry.'

But the young Briton hesitated. 'It would be difficult and dangerous. Every time I leave the fort, the guards check I am not stealing . . . but sometimes I am allowed to eat the leftovers.' She brightened with an idea. 'If you, Jenny, came with me to help, you could at least share some of them.'

'But, there's no way I could leave the boys, Edith, and anyway, I'd be too scared to come by myself.'

'Perhaps they could come too. There is always work for local men.'

'What sort of work?' asked Max, suspiciously.

'Oh, fetching and carrying and tending the latrines.'

'Latrines?'

'Toilets, Max,' said Faru from behind his hand and wrinkling his nose.

'And cleaning out the stables,' said Edith. 'There are many horses there.'

'But I don't know anything about horses.'

'You don't know much about anything, Max,' scorned Jenny, 'but that doesn't stop you thinking you do. We do need to eat though, so come on.'

'What about *Eldridge Echo*?' pointed out Faru. 'Surely someone should stay and guard it.'

'Good point, but anyone who stays here won't get fed. What do you think, Edith? Would it be safe to leave our boat?'

'I think it will be safe. There are few other boats here and I only saw yours because of the mast above the reeds.'

Jenny turned back to Faru. 'Could we lower that?'

'I think so.' He nodded to where the mast sat in a form of bracket just in front of the main cabin. 'It's meant to come down.'

'Good, let's do that then.'

While Max and Faru slackened the wire that kept the mast upright, Jenny climbed down into the dinghy. More than anything, Edith seemed fascinated by her jeans and T-shirt.

'Jenny, your tribal clothes are very strange and would make the soldiers suspicious. Better, I think, that you dress more like me. In that sack I keep spare garments in case I get wet. Help yourself.'

Thanking her, Jenny rummaged, found a rough wool cloak, and put it on before throwing the sack up to the boys. 'Here, find something for yourselves to cover your clothes or you'll stand out like sore thumbs.' She paused to take off her trainers and threw them on board. 'And leave yours too. We'll go barefoot like Edith.'

'What about our watches?' asked Faru

'Good point. Hide them down below and take mine too.'

With this done, the boys, suitably attired in concealing garments, were soon joining both girls in the dinghy, where the young Briton once more took up the rough oars and pulled away.

Up in the bow, Jenny watched *Eldridge Echo* disappear amongst the reeds and, within a short distance, they were emerging into a large body of water, much wider than she remembered the River Waveney to be.

Even though the ebb tide was helping them, the boat was moving only slowly through the water. 'I am sorry,' Edith panted, as she heaved at the oars, 'but we are many for this little boat.'

'No problem, we'll row,' offered Max, and soon the boys had swapped places and, with an oar each, were soon into their strokes and progress improved. 'So, is this *your* boat?'

'No, it is my brothers', but I love being on the water, and so they let me use it sometimes.'

Stowed along one side of the boat were some rough-hewn spars and patched cloth. 'Is that a sailing rig?' asked Faru.

'Yes. If the wind is fair, I use it to venture further into the great estuary.'

Max sniffed the breeze coming in from the sea. 'Pity we couldn't sail today. This is a heavy old boat to row.'

'But not for much longer. Look round and you'll see we're almost there,' encouraged Jenny, as the huge stone walls of the fort came into view, seemingly dominating the whole of the surrounding countryside. In spite of her apprehension, it was thrilling to think that soon they would be experiencing firsthand, something straight out of the pages of one of her history books. Getting nearer, she was in awe to see sunshine reflecting off the helmets of figures pacing the castle walls. Real Roman soldiers. Would they be friendly or was coming here just one big mistake? They would soon find out.

Chapter Four

As they got even closer, Jenny saw there was a small harbour with a wooden jetty extending out into the river. She nodded towards it. 'Right, head for that, boys.' She'd noticed a dozen soldiers gathering there to watch the boat's approach. She turned to Edith. 'Are there normally so many?'

The young Briton frowned. 'No. Perhaps they have seen your own boat and . . .'

'. . . they're waiting to arrest us,' completed Max, gloomily.

'Well, if they are, it's too late to run away now,' declared Jenny. 'All we can do is brazen it out.' She was studying the soldiers lining up on the jetty. They looked fit, disciplined and formidable in their chainmail shirts over light brown tunics, leather trousers that came to just below the knee and simple domed helmets. Short swords hung from their belts and each carried a spear, though one man held a staff with a cross-bar bearing a rectangular banner. On top of his helmet was what appeared to be the head of a wolf. '*He* looks a bit frightening,' she whispered to Edith.

'Yes, he's the *vexillarius*, and here comes their *Decurion*.'

As Max and Faru brought the boat alongside and shipped their oars, a tall soldier with the bearing of an officer was striding along the jetty barking out orders. One soldier instantly detached himself from the rest and indicated to Jenny to throw a line. She coiled the coarse rope attached to the front of the boat and threw it up. It was expertly caught and secured to a wooden post and then strong arms were heaving both her and Edith out of the boat and onto the jetty. There was an exchange between the officer and Edith, who then turned back to Jenny to explain what had been said. 'The Count's ship has been sighted in the estuary and will be here shortly. This is the honour guard and they need the jetty clear for his arrival. We must hurry into the fort to serve at the banquet.'

'But, what about the boys?'

'They must take my boat and go far away.'

'Away?' This was not in Jenny's scheme of things. 'Away where?'

'Anywhere but here . . . and quickly.'

Before Jenny could protest further, there came a rasping blare from the fort. Looking up, she saw a soldier on one of the corner towers holding a long instrument like a stretched trumpet. Its note produced immediate orders from the officer that had the guard forming into two straight lines either side of the jetty.

Edith cast a worried glance towards her boat and the boys. 'They can stay no longer. They must go . . . now!'

Without further ado, Max and Faru were simply cast off from the jetty and left to drift out into the stream, where they paused only briefly to give the girls a reassuring smile and wave. In that short time though, they had already drifted swiftly downriver with the out-going tide. Realising they were being swept away from *Eldridge*, they rowed with all their might in an effort to overcome the fast-flowing current but, making no headway at all, they soon knew that to return would be impossible until the tide turned and started coming in again.

Powerless to help, Jenny could only watch horrified as the boys accepted the inevitable, turned the boat around, and swiftly moved with the tide towards the estuary and the open sea.

She could see why. A large three-masted vessel was rounding the river's bend, moving slowly and stately under full sail towards the fort.

Another trumpet blast from the battlements had the officer bringing his men to stiff attention, before turning to salute an imposing uniformed figure making his way along the jetty to join them. Beside her, Jenny heard Edith give a little gasp. 'The garrison commander . . . come, we must go.'

As the officer barked further commands to Edith, Jenny cast a final anxious glance to where her brother and friend were already rowing past the approaching ship, before disappearing completely around the river's bend.

Edith seemed to read her thoughts. 'Have no fear. They will be back, but this is no place for us.' She took Jenny by the arm and guided her well clear of the assembling officers, along the jetty and towards a pathway. This led around the fort's high walls where sentries patrolled the parapet and others cast down suspicious glances from atop the projecting towers.

Finally, they reached the far side and the main gate, open now for the inspecting Count and with guards standing sentinel-like on either side. Before the gate and away from the fort stretched a rough track, down which were the shacks of a small settlement. The wind was easterly, carrying with it smells very different from anything Jenny had ever experienced before. She turned briefly to Edith. 'Is that your village?'

'Yes.' From the far side of the fort came the sound of more fanfares. 'But come, we must go to work,' said Edith, hustling her through the gateway.

Inside the mighty walls of the fort, Jenny suddenly felt very small and vulnerable with only Edith for company. How would she cope without Max and Faru and, perhaps more importantly, how were *they* coping alone in that tiny boat, at the will of the tide, on a wide and hostile estuary?

*   *   *

In spite of their hurried departure, the boys were coping quite well. Rowing with the advantage of a strong current, albeit in the wrong direction, they were soon passing the visiting dignitary's ship with its large square sail and a white moustache of foam creaming back from its bows. Faru guessed it to be about thirty metres long, with graceful lines that curved upwards at the stern, to end vertically as a form of shelter at the back of the ship. In front of this was a castle-like structure on which stood several figures giving orders to the men below, who were hauling on ropes to roll up the mainsail. Others were doing the same to a smaller sail on a mast angled sharply over the bows. 'It's what they call "brailing up",' explained Faru with an admiring glance. 'It's to slow the boat down for coming alongside.'

Sure enough, the wake from the Roman ship was decreasing, but still enough to roll and pitch their own small boat as it passed. For a second, Max stopped rowing to study a figure standing aloof from the rest of the officers. Clad in a burgundy-coloured robe interlaced with golden thread, his arms were folded across a chest encased in shining armour. 'He looks a bit important. Probably this Count Pomponius bloke Edith was talking about.'

Faru nodded. 'A shame he chose today to visit the fort.'

'And a shame *we* chose today to leap back eighteen centuries,' responded Max with a wry smile. He took up his oar again and pulled away. By now the ship was alongside the jetty, lines were being heaved ashore and orders shouted. Then all was lost to sight as they rounded the river's bend, while behind them, only the blare of a trumpet fanfare from the battlements marked the Count's arrival.

It was at this same time that the boys detected a change in the water. Concerned, Max looked over his shoulder and let out a cry. 'Oh no, look behind!' Completely absorbed at the spectacle of the passing ship, they had become oblivious to their whereabouts. It took only a glance now to see they were heading towards a vast body of open water that widened out into seemingly limitless sea. Already their little boat was heaving to a considerable swell and rowing immediately became more difficult.

Suddenly, everything seemed that much more threatening and Max's thoughts turned to Jenny. According to Edith, she would soon be serving the visiting dignitaries and he guessed it would be the end of the day before they could return to collect her. That seemed a long time away and he suddenly missed her and Edith very much. He took another anxious glance over his shoulder at the heaving waters ahead and noticed that the sea seemed to have blended with the sky. 'That's strange. Where's the horizon gone?'

Faru turned and studied the line of murk advancing steadily towards them. 'That's a sea-fog, Max. It's rolling in on the easterly wind.'

Even as Max gazed at this new hazard, the headlands either side of the estuary became hidden in fog and were soon lost to sight. With their drift seaward and the fog advancing, it wouldn't be long before they too were completely enveloped. A minute ago he'd been worrying about how long it would be before they could return to pick up the girls. Now he was wondering if they ever *would* return.

Chapter Five

Inside the fort, Jenny knew nothing of the approaching fog or, indeed, anything beyond her immediate surroundings as, pulling her itchy cloak tight about her, she followed Edith through the orderly lines of wooden buildings that comprised the barracks, stables and living quarters of this military camp. It was a magical glimpse into a world she had only previously read about, and she found it fascinating.

Everywhere, soldiers were busy putting a final shine on equipment or grooming their horses for the forthcoming inspection. They were all much taller than Jenny had ever imagined and looked very professional as they went about their duties. Nowhere, however, had she seen any women or children. 'Don't any of the soldiers have families?' she asked Edith.

'Not in the fort. The law prevents a soldier marrying, but many soldiers befriend local women and have families living in my village. Some choose to settle down here when their military service ends,' explained Edith as they neared an intersection at the fort's centre. She pointed ahead to two substantial buildings, much larger than the rest. 'Here are the *Praetorioum* and *Principia*.'

'The what?'

'The fort commander's quarters and the headquarters. I have often had to clean them and it is where the feast is to take place. Come, we must go through the servants' entrance.'

Jenny followed her into a side passage where young men and women, dressed in white tunics tied at the waist, scurried here and there, seemingly too intent on their tasks to notice the two new arrivals. 'Are they slaves?' asked Jenny.

'No, they are servants like you and I.' From somewhere ahead wafted the enticing aroma of cooking, and soon they were entering the kitchen where a cauldron hung suspended over an open fire, its contents bubbling. On the other side of this large room, other servants were tending a form of tiled oven while a whole headless animal carcass turned on a spit. Overseeing all was an older man with a pockmarked face and stern countenance. Seeing them enter, he came over and gave Edith some firm orders with the occasional glance at Jenny.

'We are to serve at the feast,' she relayed, when the man had left them, 'but before that we must attire ourselves like the other servants.'

Jenny followed her into a side room where cloth bags hung from wooden pegs. They contained the same sort of tunics the other servants had worn, and thong-like sandals. Taking Edith's lead, she changed into this uniform, feeling somewhat self-conscious, but hoping she was a little less conspicuous. After stuffing her jeans, T-shirt and woollen cloak into the same bag, she followed Edith back into the kitchen, the smell of cooking reminding her that she hadn't yet eaten this whole long day. Some hot food would certainly be welcome and she went over to the cauldron and took a ladle-full of the bubbling contents. 'What's in this?'

Edith took a quick glance. 'Cow's udders, peacock tongues and sheep brains.'

Jenny swallowed hard, promptly put the ladle back into the cauldron and crossed to the spit. 'Perhaps I'll stick to the roast.'

'Ah, the wild boar? That will be very nice.'

By now, a servant tending the oven was pulling out what must be the poor creature's head to anoint it with yet more oil.

'Perhaps you'd better show me where we'll be serving,' gulped Jenny, dashing from the room, her appetite replaced by a sudden sense of homesickness. She could only hope that the boys were finding their situation more palatable than hers.

*   *   *

'It's no good, Faru, it's catching up with us.'

With the fog drifting relentlessly inland, the boys had lost no time in turning the boat around and attempting to row back against the tide. It only took a glance at the last remaining features on the shore, however, to realise they were making no progress at all. 'The tide's still going out and at its strongest now,' gasped Faru, between strokes. 'If anything, we're still drifting out to sea.'

'And the fog's getting closer,' panted Max, just as aware as his friend at the futility of their effort and already feeling the clammy touch of the fogbank's edge. 'That east wind is carrying it faster than we can row.'

'The east wind!' repeated Faru excitedly. 'Of course.'

'"Of course" what?'

'The sail! We've forgotten all about the sail.' He leant down into the bottom of the boat and hauled out the mast and the long wooden spar with the old cloth furled around it. 'With this up and the wind behind us, we should make some headway.'

'Will we beat the fog?'

'I don't know, but it's worth a try. Come on, let's get it up.'

The first job was to raise and secure the mast. Once it was up, Faru was able to attach the long rope running from the top, called the halyard, to the wooden spar carrying the sail. Then he nodded towards a notch in the boat's stern. 'Right, stick your oar in that and steer the boat while I hoist this up.'

Max did as ordered, his oar now trailing from the stern, where moving it either way had the same effect as a rudder. Faru was already hauling on the halyard and raising the patched and tattered square of old cloth, which flapped noisily. 'OK, keep us running downwind so the sail fills. With a bit of luck, we can make some headway against the tide and get away from this murk.' Indeed, the fog had now caught up with them, wet, cold and clinging and with visibility down to a few metres.

'But how will I know which way to steer?' panicked Max.

'See that watery sun? Just keep that on our port side,' ordered Faru, indicating the left side of the boat. He was just tying off the halyard when his body suddenly went rigid, his ear cocked to seaward. 'What's that?'

'What's what?'

'The creak of oars. I'm sure there's another boat somewhere close.'

Max stopped trying to steer the boat and listened, first to just the sound of his own breathing and then, the unmistakable clunk and splash of several oars, followed by human voices talking in a foreign tongue. 'You're right . . .' some instinct was making him whisper, '. . . but who do you think they are? More Romans perhaps?'

But Faru was shaking his head. 'No, that's not Latin. It sounds more like German, which makes me think they might be . . .'

'. . . Saxons?' Max's heart sank as he uttered the name and a feeling of doom washed over him. 'What are *they* doing here?'

'Making a hit-and-run raid, I should think. This fog bank will give them the perfect cover.'

'Surely they're taking a chance. In this weather they could just as easily hit a sandbank or something.'

But Faru shook his head. 'Not if they've followed the wake of the Roman ship. My guess is the Saxons spotted it sailing in and took their chance.'

'If they attack the fort, Jenny and Edith could be in real danger.'

'I don't think so. I bet their plan is to raid the local village while the fort is busy with the Count's visit.'

'But that's where Edith lives! Even if she's at the

fort, her family will be there. Faru, we've got to warn them.'

'I know, but right now I think *we're* in more danger. We need to keep ahead of that Saxon ship.' He handed Max the ropes attached to each corner of the billowing sail. 'Here, you take these and I'll steer.' They swapped places and as Max hauled on the coarse ropes, the little boat seemed to surge through the water as if it too sensed the urgency of the situation. Faru concentrated on holding a straight course. Although the breeze was behind them, the tide was still running out and the water was choppy. 'How are we doing, Max? Can you see anything?'

Max allowed himself a quick glance astern, from where sinister sounds and alien voices seemed to be getting ever closer. 'Not yet, but I think they're catching us up.'

Sure enough, the image of a long, sleek ship propelled by what must have been fifteen pairs of oars was emerging from the fog. It had no sail, but doubtless the sea breeze was helping its relentless speed. In the bow stood a figure brandishing an axe, his bearded face almost hidden by a metal helmet and noseguard, his huge frame encased in chainmail and a maroon cloak. Almost scarier was his voice, a deep guttural yell that had the other tribesmen hardening their stroke and the boat slicing through the choppy water ever faster.

Max gave a yell of his own. 'They've seen us!' Clearly the Saxons wanted no stray boat warning of their raid and the look on the face of the leader left the boys in little doubt as to what would happen if they ever fell into his hands.

Despite Faru's best efforts, the enemy ship seemed to be closing the gap with frightening speed. Capture was, perhaps, just minutes away. They were two against more than thirty and there seemed no way of escape.

*   *   *

Carrying another pitcher of wine into the banqueting area, Jenny was trying hard to blend with all the other servants.

Flanked by their staff and lounging on low cushions in the headquarters' dining area, Count Pomponius and the Fort Commander sat at the head of the twenty or so officers and dignitaries sharing their feast. All were clad either in togas or military uniforms and seemed to have a huge capacity for food and drink. Jenny was shocked at such indulgence and even more at the leering glances cast in her direction, the worst coming from the Count himself.

'He is returning to Rome soon,' explained Edith, 'so this is his farewell celebration.'

Just as well, thought Jenny, as she refilled the big man's goblet for the umpteenth time and turned away from his leering eyes. Watching all the other servants scurrying back and forth with huge platters of food on their shoulders, she knew that, in spite of being similarly dressed, her taller bearing, unblemished skin and fresh clean fragrance had marked her out as un-questionably different. Though this brought admiring glances from the dignitaries, it seemed to trigger ones of jealous hostility from the servants. Finding favour with a person of rank must be a step up the serving ladder, she thought, and could understand why they resented her.

Clearly Edith thought it a gift from the gods. 'The Count likes you,' she confided excitedly as they passed between banquet and kitchen. For her part, Jenny just wished with all her heart that this experience was over and she was heading back to her own time and family, especially as the odious kitchen overseer had pulled Edith to one side, speaking in hushed tones, but with piercing glances in her direction. When he had finished, Edith quickly relayed the message. 'Count Pomponius likes you so much, he wants to keep you.'

'He *what*?' Jenny couldn't believe what she was hearing.

'Yes. When he continues on his voyage tonight, you will sail with him and then on to Rome where you will serve in his household.'

'But . . . but that's impossible.' Jenny felt the cold hand of dread seizing her in its icy grip. 'I won't . . . he can't make me.'

'He is the most important Roman in this part of Britannica, Jenny. He can do what he wants.'

'Not with me, he can't.' She glanced around frantically. 'Edith, you've got to help me get away.'

'But it's an honour, Jenny. You will be with a very important man in the empire.'

'I can't, Edith. Please, please help me.'

Just at that moment a servant passed, carrying a platter with the whole boar's head on his shoulder. He gave a gruff order and nodded towards more pitchers of wine. Honour or not, there was clearly work still to do. Reluctantly, she followed Edith back into the banqueting area but, just before they entered, the young Briton turned and whispered, 'Make this serving and then meet me by the entrance.'

Feeling near to despair, Jenny was only too glad to take these words as a sign of hope.

* * *

Hope was something Max was in short supply of right then.

'Faru, they're only metres away now.' Out on the estuary with the Saxons in hot pursuit, he was trying to keep the panic from his voice as the sleek raider came ever closer. 'Can't we sail this thing any faster?'

'Not running with the wind, we can't, unless . . .' Faru cast a glance at the tattered banner flying from the enemy ship's stern, and then straightway put the helm over to starboard. The little boat turned abruptly through ninety degrees, almost under the Saxon's bow, the sail flapping as it spilled its wind.

'What are you doing? They're almost on us and we're slowing down.'

'Not if you get that sail pulled in tighter. Quick, haul it more towards our centreline until it stops flapping.'

Max did as ordered and immediately the tattered square of cloth re-filled with wind and the boat heeled to starboard. Then he glanced back to the Saxon ship where more figures, armed with swords and axes, were gathering in the bow, clearly relishing the prospect of easy prey. But, as their ship turned to follow, it was no longer closing the gap. 'Hey, we're beating them.'

'Or at least holding our own.' Faru glanced at the healthy bow-wave creaming away on their either side. 'I reckon this is as fast as we can go.'

'It doesn't make sense to me,' frowned Max. 'I thought we'd be fastest with the wind behind us.'

'No. What we're doing now is called "reaching". Instead of blowing us along, the wind is sucking us, which is a much more powerful force. We should be at the shore very soon.'

'How do you know that? It's still completely hidden by fog.'

Faru nodded ahead to where the sun still peeked weakly through the overcast. 'That must be pretty well south, so now I'm steering straight for it.'

The Saxon crew were still rowing feverishly along the furrow of white left behind the boys' small boat. 'They're following our wake, Faru. When we reach the shore, they'll be onto us in minutes.'

'They might be onto something else first.' Faru smiled for the first time since the chase began. 'This boat probably floats in just a few centimetres of water, but theirs must need at least a metre.' He was noticing the water around them was now coloured by a muddy hue. 'I think it's getting shallower already, and my guess is that very soon . . .' But, before he could even complete the sentence, the pursuing raider suddenly veered, slowed and then came to a complete standstill, accompanied by much shouting and the clenching of fists by those on board. 'Brilliant!' exclaimed Faru, punching the air. 'They're stuck on the mud. If I keep the sun on our port side again now, we should keep parallel to the shore.'

They were running before the wind again, slightly slower, but already losing sight of the raider in the fog, its crew leaping overboard, up to their waists in water and heaving their ship in a frantic effort to refloat it.

Faru grinned. 'They'll have to be quick. The tide's still going out and, even if they get it off, they'll have to stay further out in deeper water than us. We should see the shore soon and then we'll hug it back to the fort.'

'And alert the soldiers.' They ploughed on, the shouts and groans behind fading to nothing and the only sound now, the reassuring sluice of water churning past their own hull. Just as Max was wondering if they were lost, tree-lined land slowly materialised through the murkiness. 'Great, we've made it. We must be near the fort.'

'Thank goodness for that.' Faru cocked his ear. 'I think I can hear something.' It was the eerie ringing of a bell and shouting in a Latin tongue. Then the first vague outline of the fort emerged, seemingly floating on a thin cushion of vapour, through which the jetty and Count's ship were only just visible. Once more, the sound of trumpets could be heard, but this time, more urgent, as though calling the men to arms. 'Sounds like a full-blown alert. They must have already found out the Saxons are going to attack.'

'I can't see how.' Faru was looking towards the track between the fort and the jetty. 'And what's going on there?'

Max followed his gaze and saw, not a force of cavalry galloping out to meet the enemy, but two girls, running for all their might towards the jetty and being closely pursued by a whole host of armed legionnaires. As they ran, the first girl was trying to conceal jeans and T-shirt beneath a flapping cloak. The second shorter girl was casting anxious glances over her shoulder at the soldiers hard on their heels, her uncombed brown hair flying wildly and a look of sheer terror on her face. And now, alerted by sounds of alarm, sailors from the Count's ship were jumping ashore to head them off.

Max watched in horror. 'Faru, that's Jenny and Edith . . . and something's gone horribly wrong.'

Chapter Six

After serving more wine and avoiding Count Pompo-nius's unwanted advances, Jenny had made a fast exit from the scene, hurrying towards the room where she had left her clothes and hoping the merry revellers were now too drunk to notice. Quickly changing back into her jeans and T-shirt and covering them once more with the old woollen cloak, she had made her way towards the entrance, breathing a sigh of relief when she found Edith already waiting. 'Oh, thank goodness you're here, Edith. I'm so scared.'

'Come, follow me.' With nervous glances towards the guards, Edith led her out of the building and back through the fort's military lines.

Jenny hurried after her, with occasional checks behind for any sign of the raised alarm. 'What will happen, Edith, when they find us gone?'

'Much anger.' The young girl's face was clouded with fear. 'They must not catch us, Jenny. No-one is allowed to disobey an order from the masters.'

Suddenly, Jenny realised the terrible danger in which she had placed, not only herself, but this young girl who had given her only friendship. Even if they got out of the fort undetected, where would they go then? The boys were probably still far out on the estuary and there would be no other means of escape.

And then, suddenly, there came the urgent ringing of a bell from the direction of the fort commander's quarters. Edith stopped in her tracks. 'An alarm . . . they know we have fled . . . quick!'

They set off running between the barrack huts, avoiding soldiers relaxing after their inspection, weaving between horses feeding outside their stables, and the clatter of pursuers sounding ever closer. Jenny cursed the sandals slowing her down, but stopping to shed them was not an option with the main gate so close. She prayed it would be open.

It was, but from the battlements trumpets were adding their own urgent call to arms and the guards either side of the gate were hurriedly closing them. It was now or never and before the guards could turn to stop them, both girls had fled past and out onto the fort's encircling path. For the first time, Jenny saw that the surrounding land was shrouded in fog. Perhaps that might give them enough cover to escape. Frantically trying to keep her jeans and T-shirt covered, she forged on, hot on Edith's heels towards the jetty and river, hoping against hope that the boys might just be there to rescue them.

They were almost at the jetty itself when, to Jenny's delight, she caught sight of Max and Faru looming out of the fog bank in Edith's boat, under full sail and churning towards them. But, by now, dozens of soldiers, led by the Decurion, were in hot pursuit, while ahead sailors from the Count's ship, alerted by the general pandemonium, were jumping onto the jetty to head them off. Jenny stopped running and grasped Edith's arm. 'Can you swim?'

The young Briton shook her head. 'No, but *you* must take *your* chance, Jenny. Leave me and go with the boys.'

'No way.' Jenny waved to the boat, now only metres away. Her own capture was inevitable, but perhaps she could still warn the boys off.

A forlorn hope. Soldiers and sailors were now surrounding them and strong hands grabbing their arms. Overwhelmed by the finality of defeat, Jenny felt her spirits ebbing as swiftly as the water beneath them. She turned to see Max dropping the sail and Faru steering the boat straight for the jetty and, above the jabber of her captives, tried to hear what it was they were shouting.

*   *   *

Faru brought the boat alongside, yelling as he did so. 'Let them go . . . Saxons . . . in the estuary . . . preparing to attack.'

Max threw the bow rope up to the assembled crowd. It was promptly caught and secured to a post before soldiers roughly pulled both boys out of their boat.

'Max!' shouted Jenny, struggling against the men holding her. 'You shouldn't have come back.'

'We had to.' The surrounding soldiers were now obediently parting to admit the dignified figure of the fort commander, striding along the jetty to take

55

control. Max turned to Edith. 'Quick, tell him there's a Saxon ship aground in the estuary. We came back to warn them.'

The words poured out as Edith relayed the message to the commander. After anxious glances downriver, he turned to the troop-leader and snapped out orders that sent the man running back towards the fort shouting instructions of his own.

Then another crisp order and all four youngsters were being manhandled along the same path and into the fort where more soldiers watched them in sullen silence. Managing to catch Edith's eye, Max gave her a fleeting smile before they were pushed roughly to one side as a whole troop of armed cavalry came galloping by. Shields and weapons flashing, harnesses jangling, they rode out through the gate to disappear along the eastward track in a cloud of dust. 'At least they seem to be taking our warning seriously,' he managed to mutter to Faru, as they were jostled off once more.

Soon they were on the edge of the cavalry barracks and being pushed into a small, squalid building, its filthy earth floor barely covered by straw and the only source of light, a single slit of barred window high on the outside wall. The heavy wooden door was banged shut and they were alone.

Jenny slumped down against the damp wall, unable to hold back her tears any longer. She turned to Edith. 'How could I have got you into this mess? I'm so sorry.'

Edith gave a weak smile and started to shiver. The dampness of the fog was creeping in and she still wore only her serving tunic. Max moved close to her and opened one side of his cloak, allowing her to huddle up with him for warmth. 'I'm sure we'll sort it out.' He turned back to his sister. 'But what on earth made you run like that?'

Between sobs, Jenny gave a full account of all that had happened at the banquet and the reason for their attempted escape.

'But that's awful, Jen. You must've been petrified and did right to make a run for it,' reassured Max, scowling. 'If you'd let them take you off in the ship, we'd never have seen you again.'

'I know, but now none of us might ever see *anyone* again.' She sniffed, trying hard to hold back tears. 'But what about you two? You seem to have had plenty of excitement yourselves.'

'You could say that.' Max told of their own adventure. 'I only hope they found that Saxon ship still aground. Otherwise they'll think we just made it all up.'

'The tide will have turned by now,' said Faru, 'so let's hope it didn't float off the mud before the cavalry got there.'

'I guess we'll just have to wait and see.'

By now, they'd lost all sense of time, but it must have stretched into hours before the sound of hooves, passing by the cell block, caught Max's attention. He sprang to his feet. 'Here, Faru, give me a lift up so I can see what's happening.'

His friend knelt below the slit opening while Max climbed onto his shoulders. Outside, the troop of cavalry were returning at a much slower pace than their departure, horses and men both smeared with mud and, in some cases, blood that seeped through hastily bandaged wounds. He peered wide-eyed at the scene before him. 'Wow, they must have been in a fierce old fight.'

'Seems like they found the Saxons then,' gasped Faru, beginning to buckle under his friend's weight.

Max slithered down. 'So, where does that leave us?'

The answer to that came surprisingly quickly, when the cell door was thrown open and a squad of soldiers beckoned them to stand and follow. Soon they were outside and being marched towards the fort's head-quarters. Escorted inside, they were ushered into the banqueting area where Max recognised the imposing figure of Count Pomponius sitting in regal authority at the head of the assembled officers and officials. Was this to be a form of trial or were they to be simply sentenced to some sort of horrific punishment? Edith, he noticed, had fallen to her knees, but he stayed standing as did his sister and Faru. But it was to Edith that the Count addressed his words.

When he had finished, she turned, her face a picture of relief, as she relayed all that had been said. 'Your warning was good and the raiders have been beaten. Count Pomponius said you have done the empire a service and will be rewarded, first by your freedom and also with gold.'

With that, at a snap of the Count's fingers, an official entered carrying a small leather pouch which he handed to Max. It was heavy and bulging with what felt like coins. Almost more important, though, was the sight of the servants bearing food.

Relieved, the youngsters tucked into the feast with relish, before being ushered out, feeling like heroes, as they were led through barracks where hostility had been replaced by admiration. They continued out through the gate and back to the jetty where Edith's boat still lay moored in the shadow of the Count's ship. A final salute from the troop-leader and they were alone once more to savour their change in fortune. Max opened the bag and poured the coins out onto the jetty, the gold glinting in the afternoon sun. He estimated there must be over two hundred of them, each bearing the head of an emperor.

Edith gasped. 'They are *aurei*. You are very rich.'

'But what will *we* do with Roman coins?' said Max. 'If it hadn't been for you, we would never have seen Jen again.' He turned to the others. 'I vote we keep ten and give Edith the rest.'

'Great idea,' said Faru.

'She's definitely earned them,' agreed Jenny.

So, Max pocketed ten coins before putting the rest back in the bag and handing it to Edith. 'Here, these are no good to us and we want you to have them. It'll help you and your family lead an easier life . . . and, just think, you'll be able to buy a boat of your own.'

Edith was overcome with emotion and gratitude and could barely speak. 'Oh, it is so much . . . I cannot believe it . . . we will be wealthy beyond our dreams . . . if there is anything I can do to thank you . . .'

'There is just one thing. Please will you take us back to *our* boat?'

Helped by the now-incoming tide, they were soon at the cut into the reedbeds where, much to their relief, they found *Eldridge Echo* undisturbed. There was an air of great sadness as they said their goodbyes and climbed on board, but it was Max who turned back and said, with a catch in his voice, 'I think you're terrific, Edith. I wish you could come with us, but I know this is where you belong.' He forced a smile. 'And I'm sure you can't wait to see your family's faces when you arrive home and show them your gold.'

'Thanks to you. Goodbye, Max, I will never forget you . . .' she wiped away a tear and smiled at the others, '. . . any of you.'

And then she was gone, pausing on her oars at the bend in the dyke for one last wave.

Jenny put a hand on her brother's shoulder. 'You liked her, didn't you Max?'

He did a poor imitation of a shrug. 'She was great . . .' he turned and nodded at the boat's silent data displays, '. . . but the sooner we're out of here, the better. Let's see if this thing will get us back to *our* home and family.'

Chapter Seven

'So, how do the batteries look?'

'Better than when we left them.' *Eldridge*'s wheelhouse was alive once more with backlit digital displays and humming technology. Faru turned from studying the battery state and added, 'But as they've only had charge from the solar panels, they're nowhere near back to full power.'

Jenny gave a pleading look. 'Will they get us forward to our own time?'

'I'm not sure. We've got more than seventeen hundred years to go.'

'Well, at least let's get as far as we can.' Max moved towards the power lever. 'I've had enough of the Roman Empire.'

'Even if it does mean leaving Edith behind?' teased Jenny.

Max ignored her and pushed the lever forward before Faru had a chance to do it. Immediately, the familiar whine and vibration began and a blue mist once more clouded the wheelhouse windows. All eyes though, were on the digital year gauge.

At first the figures seemed to be stuck at 279, but then, agonisingly slowly, they began advancing . . . 283 . . . 320 . . . 'We're off . . . we're on our way back,' squealed a delighted Jenny.

'Don't get too excited, folks. Remember the batteries aren't fully charged,' warned Faru. 'Throttle back a bit, Max, or they'll run down too quickly.'

Max brought the lever back a fraction, but the years were still flying past, through the five-hundreds, six-hundreds and ever faster through the seven, eight and nines but, as they approached one thousand, their speed began to suddenly slow down. Faru cast a nervous glance at the battery instruments. 'I thought this would happen. We're back into the yellow arcs and losing power.'

Sure enough, the years showing on the gauge had come to a stop, the mist was clearing and yet more marshland was appearing beneath the boat. 'Oh no! We're going down again,' cried Jenny. 'Where on earth are we *now*?'

Max looked out through the wheelhouse window. 'We seem to be landing on a wide river with reeds along the banks.'

'Which one do you think it is?'

'How would I know? They all look the same.'

There was a slight splash as *Eldridge Echo* settled onto the water and, as the whine decreased, the battery warning lights flickered and then faded.

'That's it. Power's gone,' said Faru with a sigh. 'This is as far as we're going for now.'

Jenny ran a trembling hand through her hair. 'And just when is "now"?'

All eyes went to the year gauge. Its red numbers were at 1004.

*   *   *

Max steeled himself to peer beyond the wheelhouse windows again. 'Do you think we're still on the Waveney?' he asked, as the boat, carried by the flow of the river, glided silently past reedbeds on either bank.

'Goodness knows,' replied Jenny, 'but we seem to be in the middle of nowhere, so the sooner we start charging the batteries, the better.'

'Except, I don't think we can, because they're totally dead. There's not even enough life in them to start the engine,' said Faru, glumly.

All three children looked at each other in despair until Max's face suddenly lit up. 'I've just had a thought. All the cruisers we've been on before had a separate battery just to start the engine. Perhaps this one has too. Go on, Faru, turn the key and see what happens.'

Sure enough, from below their feet came the clunk of a big engine turning over and then a few gasps of combustion as it clattered to noisy life.

'Hurray and good thinking, Max!' cried Jenny, giving her brother a pat on the back. She turned to Faru. 'How long before the batteries are charged enough for us to try again?'

'Quite a while, I should think, so it's going to be a long, hungry wait unless we find somewhere to stretch our legs and get food.'

'Well, we can't do either floating down this river,' said Max, 'so what's next?'

'If only the prof had got the engine set up to drive the boat as well as generate electricity, we could go and find out what's further up the river,' said Faru.

Max was examining the wheelhouse, hoping some magical solution to their problem might present itself, when he spotted a chrome lever just to the side of the steering wheel. 'This must be the throttle control.' Sure enough, it had AHEAD, STOP and ASTERN written on it. 'Shall I try pushing it forward and see if it does anything?'

Faru and Jenny looked at each other, shrugged shoulders and both nodded. 'OK, but gently this time,' warned Faru.

Max eased the lever forwards but, although the engine revved, the boat stayed still. 'Why doesn't it work?'

'Obviously, something's not connected.' Faru nodded down to the engine space below the wheelhouse floor. 'Shall I have a look?'

'Nothing to lose,' said Jenny.

Faru pulled up the deck plates, leaned down into the engine compartment and, after some prodding and poking, let out a modest cheer. 'I was right. The pin which joins the lever cable to the gearbox is missing.'

'Goodness, how do you know that?' asked Jenny, impressed with such knowledge.

'The hard way. My uncle's engine in Bangladesh was always going wrong.'

'Right, but can you fix this one?' asked Max.

Faru stood up and wiped his hands. 'Not without a spare pin, but all's not lost because we can hoist the sail and get somewhere while still charging the batteries?'

Minutes later, the mast and old sail were up and *Eldridge* was moving through the water and not just with it. At the wheel, Faru suggested they should go with the wind and tide and see where it took them. He turned and grinned. 'She handles well enough. So far, so good.'

'Until we meet someone.' Jenny had raised her voice above the noise of the engine. 'This racket will certainly warn people we're coming.'

'If the year's 1004, the Romans won't still be here, will they?' queried Max, anxiously.

'Of course not. They all left over five-hundred years ago. The Anglo-Saxons came as soon as they left and *they'll* be the people living here now – well, at least until the Norman conquest . . .'

'. . . in 1066,' added Max, chuffed to know at least *some* history. 'Over sixty years to go to that, so let's hope these Saxons are friendlier than the last ones we met.'

Jenny thought hard. 'Actually, it was the Angles who settled in this area, and I think they were peaceful enough.'

'Well, we'll soon know!' exclaimed Faru, pointing southwards to where a column of smoke curled upwards from beyond the reedbeds.

Max saw it too. 'Do you think it's a village, Jen?'

'Who knows, but we need food and we've got those gold coins to pay for it, so let's go and investigate. It's a good thing we're still wearing Edith's spare clothes though.'

As the source of the smoke drew closer, they could see a few crude houses on the river's edge, small and round with thatched pitched roofs on top of low, rough-looking walls. Jenny turned to Faru 'You'd better stop the engine. We don't want to scare the locals.'

With the engine shut down, the silence was broken only by the sound of ringing. 'Is that a bell?' muttered Max.

But, as they reached the settlement, Jenny caught sight of a figure between the houses, drawing a bar of metal from a blazing fire and striking it with a hammer. 'No, look, it's a blacksmith at work. Steer the boat to the bank over there, Faru.'

As *Eldridge* nosed into the grassy shore, the man stopped his hammering and gazed in amazement. He was big and muscular, wearing woollen leggings, open sandals and a rough tunic of grey cloth, held at the waist with a leather belt. He stood frowning, scratching his unkempt beard, before striding slowly towards *Eldridge*, his hammer still held menacingly at the ready. Just metres away, he stopped, casting suspicious glances towards them, saying nothing, but scowling threateningly. As he stood there, a small cluster of women and children gathered nervously in the distance. Jenny took a deep breath and whispered to the boys, 'Oh well, here goes.' She opened the wheelhouse door and forced a confident smile.

There was no smile in return. 'Who are you?' The words were in English, if slightly guttural.

'We have come from Burgh Castle,' Jenny answered truthfully. 'Can you help us, please? We need food.'

'You are not Danes?'

'No, we're English like you.'

The man seemed to relax, but stepped forward and, without warning, raised his hammer. Jenny flinched until she realised he was bringing it down with a ringing clout on *Eldridge*'s hull. 'What metal is this?'

'A sort of iron,' she answered.

'But, it is like nothing from here. I am a blacksmith and I cannot make things like this. How does iron float? It cannot be.' He shook his head, puzzled. 'And you do not look like us, though you say you are from our country.'

'But, a distance away,' explained Jenny. Eager to stop more questioning, she held out her hand in friendship. 'I'm Jenny and this is Max and Faru.'

A grimy hand took hers in a strong, firm grip. 'I am Gareth. You say you need food?'

It was Max who spoke up to explain they had travelled a long way in search of something to eat. 'If you can spare us any, we have money.'

The man took one more bewildered look at *Eldridge* and nodded towards the nearest house from which more smoke coiled upwards from a hole in the roof. 'We have none to sell, but if you are hungry you are welcome to share what little we have.'

The three youngsters scrambled down from the boat, thanking the man profusely as they followed him back to his forge.

'I am a metalworker. I make tools,' explained Gareth as they tucked into some meagre cold chicken pieces and raw vegetables. He picked up the bar he had been hammering and Jenny could see it had the makings of a heavy sword.

She frowned. 'You make weapons too. Who needs weapons, Gareth? Who is the enemy?'

He glanced eastwards towards the unseen sea. 'The Danes.'

Max could sense fear in this big man's voice. 'You mean the Vikings?'

'Yes, the dreaded Northmen.'

'Are they still raiding then?'

Gareth nodded, sadly. 'Only this last two years since our king, Ethelred, stopped paying gold for protection and, on Saint Brice's Day, ordered the killing of all Danes still in this country. One of those killed was the sister of Sweyn Forkbeard, the Danish king, and last year he started invading our country in revenge.'

'So, are the Danes back here in East Anglia?' asked a nervous Jenny.

'Not yet, but we live in fear that any day their blood-thirsty hordes might bear down upon us.'

'Which is why you're busy making swords,' said Max, feeling the sharp edge of the weapon and glancing around at the remoteness of their location. 'Do you sell them here?'

'No, they are sold in the town of Norvic. By law, any goods worth more than twenty pennies have to be sold in the town.'

'Norvic must be Norwich,' said Jenny to the boys, before turning back to Gareth. 'So where are we now?'

'This is the settlement of Bramerton. It is just a quarter day's ride to the town.'

'Could we buy food there?'

'Oh yes, it has a big market and my daughter, Megan, is taking some of my goods there this very morning. You could join her if you wish.'

'Not walking, I hope,' said Max, frowning.

'No, I have a horse and cart. Megan has gone to fetch it from a farmer close by. She will return soon.'

At last, a bit of good luck, thought Jenny. 'Great.' She turned to the boys. 'Are you up to hitching a ride into Norwich . . . Norvic . . . with her?'

But Faru, studying the forge, had other ideas. 'I was just wondering . . .' He turned to the blacksmith, '. . . if you could make us a part.'

'A "part"?'

'Yes, just a small pin for our boat. We'll pay you.'

The big man shrugged. 'If it is of iron, then I can make it.'

Faru turned back to Jenny. 'An iron pin would be better than nothing. Why don't I stay here and show Gareth what we need while you and Max go to Norwich to get food?'

Jenny wasn't keen on the idea of splitting up, but realised it made sense. 'OK, but keep close to *Eldridge*, Faru.'

By now, a young girl had arrived at the forge with the horse and cart. 'This is my daughter Megan,' introduced her father, proudly, as he loaded up his goods.

Despite the simple cloak fastened with a cord, dark hair dangling in dirty tangles, unwashed feet and a strong body odour, she had a familiar-looking face. Staring open-mouthed, Max stammered, 'B . . . but, you're not Megan . . . you're Edith.'

*   *   *

As horse and cart trundled them along close to the river bank towards Norwich, Jenny's thoughts turned to home and family. She put her arm around Max and spoke quietly. 'I wonder what Mum and Dad are doing now? They must be out of their minds with worry about us.'

'We'll get home one day soon, Jen. There's nothing more we can do, so let's just get on with it.'

A light breeze was rippling the surface of the water where small skiffs and larger square-rigged trading boats passed to and fro. It was the River Yare that the twins and Megan were trundling beside, following a winding trail through glades of overhanging trees that filtered the morning sun. In this peaceful setting, Jenny thought it was time to find out a little more about this girl who bore such an uncanny resemblance to the Briton, Edith.

'Have you a mother, Megan?'

'No, she died when I was born, so it is just me and my father.'

Seated beside her, Max leaned back to finger one of several new weapons lying on the floor of the cart. 'You must be a great help to him.'

'I try, but I am sure a son would have been a greater blessing. At least the money I get for these will buy more iron for Father's forge.'

Talk of money triggered another of Jenny's concerns. 'Will the market take our gold coins for food?'

Megan smiled. 'Of course. Norvic mints its own money, but gold is very valuable.'

The track had brought them back to a small wooden bridge that crossed the river. Once on the other side, they passed through a hamlet of crude houses where inhabitants stared and dirty children played amongst the squalor of roaming dogs, pigs and poultry. Max was holding his nose and trying to hide his disgust as he asked, 'Is this Norvic?'

'No, Norvic lies on the River Wensum which joins this river. We are nearly there.'

Sure enough, another mile brought them to the outskirts of a far larger settlement, and soon they were lurching along narrow littered streets bustling with crowds of people carrying on their daily life. On either side, tradespeople were selling their wares. Outside one building a butcher was hacking at a large animal carcass while, in another, a carpenter was working a pedal lathe, the sweet smell of sawdust mingling with the aroma of fresh bread from the baker's oven next door. The latter made Jenny realise just how hungry she was. 'How much further 'til we get to the market, Megan? I'm starving.'

'We are very close now. It is on a bend in the river where the trading ships tie up.'

Sure enough, in another quarter mile, Megan was guiding the horse through crowded stalls selling everything from fruit and vegetables to cloth and jewellery. She finally stopped beside one piled high with assorted pots, pans, tools and a few weapons, behind which a tiny man in a funny pillbox cap and leather apron, smiled and came out to greet her. 'This is Orvin, the ironmonger. He buys my father's goods. I must spend time with him now to get the best price.'

'Right, we'll leave you to it and have a look around,' said Jenny, jumping down from the cart. 'Come on, Max, FOOD!'

They stayed close together, avoiding the many beggars and marvelling at wealthier men in tunics of finer cloth and leather, and ladies in stylish cloaks fastened with glistening brooches and bejewelled cuff clasps. Jenny noticed some wore leather belts with money pouches, a knife and often a set of large keys. Megan had explained earlier that these were called "girdle hangars" and showed the wearer owned a house.

'But how on earth can people put up with this stink?' grumbled Max, burying his nose in the bend of his elbow. 'No wonder people died young. What do you think is running along these open gullies, Jen? It smells like a sewer.'

Jenny could only agree and promised she would never complain about the state of public loos again. 'I wonder if Gareth's been able to make the pin for Faru? He certainly seemed overjoyed with the gold coin we gave him.'

'Life must be hard, bringing Megan up by himself,' said Max. 'She's a lovely girl, but isn't it freaky that she looks just like Edith? They've even got the same brown eyes.'

'Yes, that's very odd,' agreed Jenny, 'but just a coincidence. Anyway, let's find something to eat before we starve.' They'd stopped beside a stall piled high with flat loaves of bread. 'These will go down well.'

Having paid a gold *aureus* for four loaves, and haggled some silver and bronze Norvic coins in change, they moved on, hungrily munching the bread, and stopping at another stall for some cheese to eat with it. Drink was more of a problem. All they could buy tasted like watered-down beer.

'What I'd give for a bag of crisps and a coke,' moaned Max.

'Yes, well at least this won't rot our teeth. Let's find somewhere less crowded to eat the rest, away from this smelly market.'

Making their way through the labyrinth of stalls, they eventually found themselves in an open area where a group of young musicians were playing a cheerful tune on wooden instruments unlike any they'd seen before. 'How about here?' suggested Jenny, until she looked behind her and saw a wizened little man with a performing bear, continuously prodding the poor chained creature with a sharp stick every time someone stopped to watch it dance.

Max moved them on. 'Just accept it, Jenny. These are cruel times.'

'I know that, but living in them is very different to reading about them in the comfort of our own home.' They were still near the edge of the market, but something was happening in the town centre that made her grip her brother's arm. 'Max . . . look . . . it's on fire!'

Sure enough, dark clouds of smoke were rising above flames leaping high into the air. Within seconds, the twins were horrified to hear shrieks and cries as hundreds of people stampeded in panic towards them.

'They're escaping this way.' Max grabbed her arm. 'Jenny, RUN!'

Already, the first of the fleeing townsfolk were flooding into the market shouting the same dreaded word. 'Danes!'

'My God, Max, it's the Vikings!' Jenny grabbed a young lad colliding against her. 'What's happening?'

He turned, his face a mask of smoke, dirt and fear. 'It is Sweyn Forkbeard . . . come to burn the city and kill us all.' He wriggled free of Jenny's grasp and fled into the surging crowd.

'Max, we have to escape.'

Her brother glanced into the market where bodies were being trampled on and stalls overturned in the crush of charging people. 'But what about Megan? We can't leave her here. We've got to help her. Come on.'

Grabbing Jenny's hand, he was off, darting amongst the chaos and pushing aside anyone unfortunate enough to get in his way.

Jenny was dragged behind, hoping and praying they would be in time to rescue Megan. As they fled, she heard high-pitched screams coming from behind. She glanced round and saw the bear, free of its chains, clawing and trampling its owner before pursuing a group of terrified women further into the human frenzy. A yank from Max turned her attention back to their own fight for survival and she ran on.

And then they were close by the ironmonger's stall and shouting for Megan.

'I'm here.'

They both looked frantically for the source of this frightened voice and saw a white face peering from beneath the trestle-table. Megan shakily scrambled to her feet and fell into Max's arms. 'I was afraid the crowd would crush me and so I hid under there.' She was distraught. 'My father's goods . . . they are stealing them all.'

'Forget them. We have to escape. Are there *any* weapons left?'

'Just these, that I grabbed before hiding.' She handed across a short sword and wooden-handled knife.

'Good. What about the horse and cart?'

'The horse took fright and bolted.'

'Probably useless now anyway, but we need to get out of here and fast.'

Jenny looked at the terrified mob, in wild disarray and still flooding down from the town, pursued by large figures in metal helmets, wielding broad swords and axes and yelling hideous cries of war and retribution. 'The Vikings, Max! They'll be among us any minute now.'

Her brother took only a second to decide. 'The river. We'll make a dash for there and perhaps we can find a boat to escape in. Come on.'

Once again he took off at a run, Megan's hand in his, the sword in his other and Jenny close behind. Ahead were the masts of trading ships and soon they found themselves breathlessly running into the port area, its wooden jetties piled high with coils of ropes, stacked barrels and all manner of other nautical clutter.

The three of them peered down to the water, desperate to find a suitable craft in which to make their escape, but all the vessels were too big and appeared to have been abandoned, except for the largest ones of all. These were long, low ships with single masts, their black clinkered hulls sweeping up to curving bows, on top of which sat dragon figureheads. Far from being abandoned, they had crews of blond-haired giants wielding swords and axes and now storming up the jetty yelling blood-curdling battle cries.

Jenny found herself paralysed with fear, sick in the knowledge that they'd run straight into the arms of the very men from whom they were trying to escape. With their own fate seemingly sealed, she still had time to worry if Faru, exposed on Forkbeard's river route to Norwich, had fallen into these same merciless hands.

Chapter Eight

Back in the Bramerton settlement, Faru and Gareth had watched in horror as the Viking fleet came storming up the Yare.

After the twins' departure with Megan, they'd been working on the replacement gearbox pin. It had taken some coaxing to get the blacksmith to board *Eldridge*, but once there, Faru had been able to show him just what was needed. At first, Gareth had been utterly confounded by the boat's engine and electronic gadgetry, but then his fascination for all things metal had taken over, and he had applied himself to the job in hand. Back at the forge, a small piece of iron had been selected and then heated and beaten until thin enough to fit through the small holes linking the throttle cable to the gearbox selector. By late morning it was finished and, excitedly, the two were anxious to take it back to the boat to try. It was just as they were about to re-board that the blacksmith had glanced downriver and seen, in the distance, a sight long-feared.

'Ye gods! The Danes! They are coming!'

Faru's eyes followed the blacksmith's shaking finger

and saw for himself the fleet of longships advancing upriver with frightening speed, their black hulls creaking as hundreds of warriors pulled steadily with long oars against the freshening wind. It didn't take Gareth's words or the dragon heads mounted high on the curving prows to tell him he was witnessing the mother of all Viking raids.

'Sweyn Forkbeard . . .' muttered Gareth, unable to control the fear in his voice, '. . . heading for Norvic to attack our town.'

'. . . and where Jenny, Max and Megan will already be!' Faru gripped the man's arm. 'Gareth, we have to do something to help them.'

But the blacksmith already had a look of defeat. 'What can *we* do against so many?'

Faru glanced desperately about him. 'Well, to start with we can get *Eldridge* off the main river and out of sight. Come on, let's pull her into the dyke.' He was indicating the narrow channel cut into the river's bank that led further into the settlement. By now, other villagers were gathering, whimpering and seemingly frozen into inertia by the raider's approach.

Pulling himself together, Gareth rallied them. 'Here, do not just stand there awaiting your fate. Take these ropes.' Soon the steel boat was being pulled into a sheltered haven just behind the houses and out of sight of the approaching Viking fleet.

Even with the wind against them, Faru estimated the longships were still making a good six knots under oars alone. He looked at Gareth, who was standing firm, and shouted at him, 'What should we do . . . run for cover like the others, or grab swords ready to fight?'

But Gareth simply shook his head. 'They will not waste time on our small settlement.'

And he was right, for the whole fleet creamed past without pause, their wash carrying into the dyke and causing *Eldridge* to pitch and roll slightly as if in protest at this cruel invasion.

Only when the last longship had disappeared around the next bend in the river, did Faru breathe again and urge more action. 'Gareth, we must fit the pin and see if we can help my friends and Megan.'

But the blacksmith put his head in his hands, despairingly. 'It will be too late, Faru. The town will be in the hands of those barbarians before we can get there.'

'But we can't just stay here and do nothing. They might spot the fleet before it reaches the town and hide until the coast is clear. We *must* find them.' He gripped the blacksmith's arm. 'Come on, I need to fit that part.'

With grim determination, they went back on board *Eldridge* and, thankfully, the pin fitted perfectly. 'A brilliant job, Gareth, but let's see if it works. Now, when I turn this key you may want to cover your ears, because there'll be a lot of noise. You won't believe what happens next, but, trust me, you'll come to no harm, and it may be our last chance to help your daughter.'

With little other option, Gareth stood, hands over his ears, in speechless wonder as *Eldridge*'s diesel engine sprang to immediate, but noisy, life.

*   *   *

'I should've realised they'd use their ships to block any escape.' Huddled in the stern of the longship with one arm around his sister and the other around Megan, Max was angry with himself for being so stupid.

'It could be worse.' Jenny gave a weak smile. 'At least we're still alive and haven't been viciously slaughtered like all those poor townsfolk.'

Looking towards the still-burning remains of Norvic, Max knew his sister was right. An ominous silence had descended on the town, broken only by the occasional scream, as the raiders mopped up their grim conquest.

Certainly, their own deaths had seemed just as certain when the Viking crew had captured them. But instead, the long-haired rugged warriors had dragged them back to their ship where one particularly evil-looking Dane stood guard, threateningly fingering the sharp blade of his battleaxe. Max's mind flashed back to the Viking Warrior game he'd loved playing on his iPad. Never again, he thought – not after the real-life violence he'd just witnessed. He turned to Megan. 'What do *you* think they'll do to us?'

The young girl shrugged her thin shoulders. 'I don't know, Max, but the Danes do take young prisoners back to their country as slaves.' Indeed, as if to confirm that this might well be their fate, there was a momentary commotion as at least thirty captured young men and women were herded along the jetty, up the gangplank and on board the longship, under the brutal eyes of as many Vikings. Stumbling close behind came yet more raiders, much the worse for drink and carrying sacks and caskets of assorted loot, which they dumped onto the deck with triumphant cries.

Jenny nodded towards a tall imposing figure jumping on board after the others, his shoulders thick-set beneath a red smock and fur cloak, one hand resting on a belted broadsword, the other holding a huge axe, its shining blade dripping an ominous red. Between elaborately winged helmet and a greying beard that stretched to his chest, his flashing eyes, set in a face streaked with sweat and smoke, were the cruellest that Max had ever seen. As if in answer to his unspoken question, one of the male prisoners gasped and muttered, 'It's Sweyn Forkbeard himself . . . God help us.'

Raising high his battleaxe, this King of Denmark jumped athletically onto a stowed barrel, shouted a battle-cry of triumph, and was answered by a rousing roar from his warriors below. More kingly commands followed, and Max turned to a young prisoner nearby who seemed to have followed the gist. 'What's he saying?'

The young man's face was a mixture of fear and defeat, as he whispered back, 'With Norvic destroyed, they plan to march on Thetford, and he needs his best men for that fight. We are to man this ship back to Denmark with his stolen treasure.'

Well, that explains why our lives were spared, thought Max. But it was small comfort for his sister.

'Denmark!' Jenny turned desperately to her brother. 'Max, we can't let ourselves be taken to Denmark. We'll never see Mum and Dad again. We have to get back to *Eldridge* and our own time.'

'I know, and we will. Don't give up, Jenny.'

As more looted food and supplies were being bundled aboard their ship, Forkbeard leapt back ashore to join his awaiting warriors. Then the lines were let go. Clearly, the King of Denmark wanted his ill-gotten treasure away from Norwich without delay. With the longship sidling away from the quay, the young male prisoners were brutally forced onto the oarsman's benches and ordered to row. Thankfully, Max wasn't amongst them and Jenny squeezed his hand. 'Perhaps they think you're too young.'

'More likely I'm being kept in reserve until one of the other rowers flakes out.' Watching the master crack his whip across the back of a sickly-looking youth, Max thought that time would not be long coming.

Despite cries and groans from the prisoners, many of whom already bore wounds, they were soon clear of the smoke-shrouded town and out into open country, with the longship cleaving along the river at a pace that only deepened Max's foreboding. 'At this rate we'll be out to sea in just a few hours . . .' he glanced up to the masthead where the long pennant had begun to stream out ahead, '. . . and even quicker with this breeze behind us.'

This fair wind had not gone unnoticed by the long-ship's master who, with yells and blows, was herding the rowers off their benches to man the coarse rope halyard running down the single mast, its lower end at-tached to the long spar that lay along the ship's length. Now it was rising as the prisoners, groaning under the continuous lash of whips, hauled it and its red and white striped sail to the masthead. As the sail billowed out, it swung across the ship's beam, catching the full force of the breeze and thrusting the longship's elegant hull ever faster eastwards. Max watched with dismay as their foaming wake furrowed behind. He whispered to Jenny, 'We'll be at sea in no time. We've got to escape . . . now or never.'

'But how?'

'The only way possible. By jumping overboard and swimming for the bank.' He glanced along the length of the ship to where the prisoners, under the Vikings' orders, were manning ropes controlling the sail. Like all rivers, the Yare was meandering its way to the sea, and trimming the sail seemed to be a continuous operation. Meanwhile, the female prisoners were simply standing around in a state of shock. The only warrior now at the stern, where the youngsters were crouched, was the helmsman, firmly grasping the right-angled tiller of the steering oar as he guided the vessel along the river's course. 'Most of the crew seem to be well forward. If we could keep them there we'd stand a chance. What we need is some sort of diversion.'

Jenny was scanning ahead, downriver, beyond the curving prow and dragonhead, to where the river was making another lazy meander. It was then she picked out a distant sound above the creaking and straining of the rigging. She shook her brother's shoulder and whispered excitedly, 'Max, can you hear what I can hear?'

Cocking his ear and listening intently, a wide grin spread across his face. 'A diesel engine. It has to be . . .'

They clutched each other in anticipation as the longship rounded the next bend and then their spirits soared as they took in the sight before them.

'Megan! . . . look there . . .' pointed out Max, eagerly. 'I think we've got our diversion!'

*　　*　　*

As *Eldridge* motored up the Yare, sail stowed and bow-wave curling away on either side, Gareth was fixated by the moving parts pushing them along. 'An iron boat that floats and moves without sails or oars,' he kept muttering.

Faru though, had already decided not to attempt an explanation. 'Take your eyes off the engine, Gareth, and use them to watch for the others. They may be escaping back to Bramerton with the horse and cart by now.'

And so they continued upriver without talking, alert to any danger that might confront them, but not quite sure what their plan of action might be once they reached Norvic.

As tree-lined banks started to replace marshland, a smell of burning filled the air and the two of them looked ahead with foreboding. They did indeed seem to be too late. With all hope fading, they were just debating whether to carry on when they both froze at a sight neither expected. Rounding the bend ahead was a black-hulled longship, its striped sail spread before the wind.

'Lord preserve us,' muttered Gareth. 'A Dragonship coming *downriver*. We must flee.'

'No.' Faru's initial instincts had been the same, but some sixth sense made him pause. The Vikings would surely be totally bewildered at the sight of *Eldridge* and, if he could take advantage of their confusion and motor at full-speed straight past, there was no way the longship could be turned in the narrow river in time to pursue them. Grabbing the binoculars from their shelf, he focussed on the approaching ship, relaying to Gareth all he was seeing.

'It's got a lot of people on board, but some look like ordinary citizens.' He lowered the binoculars and turned to the blacksmith. 'What does that mean?'

'They must be chosen prisoners, spared from being massacred to become slaves.'

Faru shook his head sadly and looked again at this wide-beamed vessel bearing down on them. 'I can see warriors standing up in the bow . . . they've obviously seen us and look pretty confused, but certainly not friendly . . . some of the prisoners are at the stern . . . hang on, someone's just fallen overboard . . . and now the ship's turning towards the bank . . . what's happening? . . . there's some sort of commotion going on and a girl's waving something at us . . . oh goodness . . . I can't believe it . . . it's . . .' he refocused the binoculars to ensure he wasn't imagining things, '. . . it's Jenny!'

*   *   *

'Good old Faru must have got the engine going and set off to rescue us.'

On the longship, Max jumped excitedly onto one of the rowing benches for a better view and saw that a whole host of Viking warriors were gathering in the bow, their prisoners behind, and all bemused by the apparition before them. 'This is our chance. Let's go for it.' He glanced towards the Viking helmsman, straining like the others to see what strange craft was approaching. 'He's the warrior who'll try and stop us,' Max whispered to the girls, 'so, when I give the order, we all need to give him a good shove over the side. Weighed down with that chain mail, he won't float and he probably can't swim anyway. How about you, Megan? Are you up for it?'

She nodded nervously. 'Of course, Max. I will do as you ask.'

'Good.' By now there was further uproar as even more Vikings joined the others in the bow. 'OK, girls . . . get ready . . .' Just behind them, the steersman, unable to leave his post, was still peering ahead. 'Right . . . now!' All three leapt straight to the stern and, before the startled Viking could defend himself, gave a co-ordinated push that sent him flying and yelling over the low gunwale and into the grey waters of the Yare, where he made a pitiful unheard cry before disappearing beneath the surface. Max grasped the steering oar and gave a firm push. Surprisingly sweetly, the longship swung her sleek bows towards the riverbank.

Still breathless from what they had done, Jenny could only gasp, 'Max . . . what are you doing?'

'Running the ship aground. While it's stuck in the mud on this side of the river, we can swim to the other bank.'

Megan's face fell. 'But I cannot swim.'

Those words immediately changed everything as Max realised that this was the one thing he hadn't checked. With his plan scuppered, there was no other way to escape. Up in the bow, the Vikings were already drawing their swords and racing towards them, alert to a danger greater than the approaching boat. But some other trouble was also erupting. 'Jenny, look, the other prisoners . . . they're fighting back.'

Sure enough, seeing their captors suddenly preoccupied, the prisoners, with vengeful screams, were tearing up planks, grabbing oars and even sacks of loot - anything that could be used as a weapon against the men who had slaughtered their families and destroyed their town. One Viking, racing towards the stern, was instantly felled and his sword taken up by a prisoner who, with one stroke, sliced at the main halyard, causing the sail on its heavy yard to come hurtling down in a tangle of crashing timber, flapping cloth and snaking ropes. From beneath this jumble of rigging came the cries of Viking warriors crushed beneath while others, further forward, bellowed oaths of fury and swore vengeance. They seemed all set to retaliate when the longship's clinkered bow ran aground with a jolt and slithered to a stop.

Max looked around desperately. Although the bow was close enough to the bank for Megan to jump ashore, there were still enough fighting Vikings up front to make a leap to safety impossible. 'Jenny, you jump over the side and swim for the other bank.'

'But what about you?'

'I'm going to stay with Megan. I can't just abandon her.'

But Jenny had no intention of going it alone and shook her head. 'No way, Max. Perhaps we can all escape together if we get *Eldridge* to come alongside.' Pulling off her cloak, she jumped up onto the longship's gunwale and waved it frantically over her head.

As if in answer, *Eldridge*'s bow wave foamed even whiter.

'Faru's seen us . . . *Eldridge* is speeding up . . .' She glanced at the pandemonium in front of her. The prisoners, full of loathing and with nothing to lose, were clearly prepared to fight to the death, but, even so, the armed Vikings seemed to be regaining the advantage, '. . . but will he get here in time?'

'I'm not sure.' Max was watching *Eldridge*'s approach, fearful that once alongside, the Vikings would board and capture it. 'Jen . . . hang on . . . its turning.'

For, in just those last seconds, *Eldridge*'s steel bow had turned away before swinging back around, to drive at full speed, straight into the longship's side planks. There came the crash of splintering wood and the rush of water surging into the hull as the longship heeled to starboard, causing everything not tied down, including many of the Vikings' weapons, to go tumbling into the lower gunwale. The prisoners, consumed with hate and bent on revenge, eagerly seized them and wasted no time in settling scores. Anxious to spare the girls the gruesome sight of slaughter, Max grabbed them both and struggled through the chaos towards *Eldridge*'s bow, still wedged hard in the longship's side.

'Max . . . I must . . .' Megan had paused to grab something from the deck before Max dragged her over the side and onto *Eldridge*. Jenny followed and as Max leapt down to join them he yelled, 'Quick, Faru! Back away!'

There was an instant vibration as the engine went astern, more splintering of wood from the stricken longship, a gradual widening of the gap between the two vessels and a cry of triumph from the prisoners holding aloft captured Viking weapons dripping with blood.

'Look, they've done it!' Jenny shouted, excitedly. 'Shall we see if they need any help?'

Already *Eldridge* was swinging around, back down-river. Behind them there were splashes as chain-clad Vikings were thrown bodily into the water while, on the longship's landward side, looted treasure was jettisoned onto the nearby bank. Max shook his head. 'Not likely. Remember, Forkbeard's still in Norwich and when he gets wind that his ship's been wrecked and all his looted treasure taken back, he'll not be best pleased. We need to get to safety, and fast. And don't worry about the prisoners. They'll know where to hide until the coast is clear and be a lot richer too.'

'Thanks to you, Max,' said Megan, taking him by surprise with an unexpected hug.

Max was just thinking how nice that felt when a burly, bearded figure came out of the wheelhouse.

Letting go, Megan flew into her father's arms and sobbed with joy at the reunion she thought would never happen.

The twins eased past and into the wheelhouse to greet the smiling figure at the helm. Jenny flung her arms around Faru's neck while Max slapped him warmly on the back. 'Were we glad to see you. You certainly saved the day . . .' From the wreck of the longship behind them, came the rousing cheer of victorious prisoners, '. . . for all of us.'

Their young friend smiled modestly, 'I could see things getting a bit tricky and knew that I needed to take desperate measures to save you.' He tapped *Eldridge*'s metal side. 'Luckily, it's a tough old boat.'

'It needed to be.' Max glanced towards the instrument panel. 'Are the batteries charged?'

'Not completely. We've only been running an hour or so.'

'But is there enough to power us ahead in time?'

'At least some of the way.'

'Well, that's better than nothing. It's definitely too dangerous to stay here with Forkbeard on the rampage.' Max went back out on deck where father and daughter still stood hugging each other. 'Megan, we have to get away, but you could come with us if you'd like to.'

Her eyes filled with tears. 'Max, I can't.' She gave her father an extra squeeze. 'I'm all he has and I can't leave him.'

'But your dad can come as well.'

Gareth stepped forward. 'I know not where you voyage in your so-strange boat, Max, but I have little doubt the Vikings will soon rule this country. Many hardships lie ahead and my place is here with my countrymen.'

Jenny came and took her brother's arm. 'Try to understand, Max. They wouldn't be happy sharing our modern life.' She nodded towards Bramerton, just coming into view. 'We want to get back to *our* home, but this is *theirs* and where they belong.'

Megan stepped forward. 'Jenny's right, Max, and we will survive even better than before – look . . .' She took an object from beneath her cloak. It was a bejewelled golden chalice, '. . . this will make us rich.'

'So that's what you stopped to grab just as we went to jump ship.' Max could only smile. 'Good for you, Megan.'

Ten minutes had father and daughter ashore, Faru skilfully backing *Eldridge* once more into midstream and Max standing in the bow waving. Across the ever-widening gap, a small figure, arm-in-arm with her father, waved back.

Jenny joined her brother and sympathised. 'I know, Max, we're *all* going to miss her.'

He nodded back and gave a heartfelt sigh. 'Yes, and now we'll never see her again.'

Further anguish was broken by a shout from the wheelhouse doorway. 'You two ready to try another time-slip?'

'You bet.' As Faru swung *Eldridge* round, Jenny went back along the deck to join him, but Max lingered a few seconds more for a last glance astern.

By now the boat was curving around yet another bend in the river and the hamlet would be lost to sight. Max joined the others in the wheelhouse. 'OK, let's go.'

Chapter Nine

'But, we've only moved forward two-hundred years!' As *Eldridge* settled back to earth and the whine of her time motors wound down, Jenny looked with dismay at the year gauge showing a disappointing 1209.

'I know.' Faru brought the time lever back to neutral and flicked the electrical master switch. 'Obviously the batteries need to be fully powered to get us the whole way back.'

With the blue mist already clearing, Max was peering out of the wheelhouse windows at yet more marshland, shrouded in early morning fog. 'I wonder where we are now?'

Jenny peered over his shoulder. 'Still in Broadland, by the look of it . . .' she glanced at the year-gauge again and thought hard, '. . . and I suppose King John must still be on the throne.'

'Wasn't he was the one who signed the Magna Carta?' asked Faru, who was beginning to find history almost as interesting as science.

'That's right.'

'Well, Robin Hood didn't think much of him,'

joined in Max. 'I know that from watching "Prince of Thieves" on TV.'

Jenny gave an exasperated sigh and put her hands on her hips. 'You do know, don't you, dear brother, that Robin Hood's just a legend? He didn't really live in Sherwood Forest and rob the rich to give to the poor.'

'Err, yes, of course I know he wasn't real,' said Max, with perhaps just a tinge of disappointment. 'So, didn't he really fall in love with Maid Marian?'

'NO, Max!'

'Hey, you two, we've got more important things to worry about,' intervened Faru. 'I still think it's too risky to recharge batteries using the engine until we know who's about, so we'll just have to rely on the solar panels.'

'Oh no, not again,' complained Jenny, shaking her head in dismay. 'Poor Mum and Dad must be going crazy wondering what's happened to us.'

'Not to mention Professor Hazlelade, who probably thinks we've nicked his boat for good,' added Max.

'Oh Max, if only you'd done as you were told, and left things alone,' said Jenny, despairingly.

'Yes, well I didn't and we can't change it, so now we have to concentrate on keeping ourselves alive and not letting any harm come to *Eldridge* so we can get home again.'

'Which means we need to camouflage the boat and then go and find some food and drink,' said Faru.

Still in their borrowed cloaks, they clambered onto the rather squelchy marshland beside the hidden channel in which *Eldridge* had come to rest. Covering the cabin roof with rushes and leaves, they made sure to leave the solar panels clear. Max managed to uproot an alder sapling to fix to the stern and tied a bit of rag to the top, before securing the wheelhouse door. 'This'll help us find it again when we return.'

They stood back to admire their handiwork before looking around for any sign of a path which might lead to habitation. There was none but, beyond the channel, the riverbank seemed firm enough to walk along, and following the course of the river seemed the best option.

'Any idea what time it is?' asked Jenny.

Faru glanced just above the horizon to where rays of light shone through the fog, now thinning into translucent mist. 'The sun's still low, but rising in the east, so we know it's early morning and what direction we'll be heading in.'

With that reassurance, they set off, following the river south and then south-east, the water just starting to ripple in the first breath of the early morn. Max slowed to watch a swan glide past. 'I wonder which river *this* is. I don't recognise it, do you, Jen?'

'No, I don't, but it's certainly narrower than the Yare. I hope we're still somewhere on the Broads.'

'And that we can find some food soon.' Max was realising for the first time in his life what real hunger felt like, when he heard a sound. 'Hang on . . . what was that?'

They'd all heard it, the creaking of timbers and voices coming from the misty marshes behind them. They turned in time to see the mast of a large boat gliding ghost-like behind the river's last meander.

'It's coming this way.' Jenny wasn't sure whether to be afraid or excited.

Max turned to her. 'Vikings?'

'Don't be silly, Max,' she scoffed. 'The last Vikings were thrown out of this country a hundred and fifty years ago, so don't panic, this can't be a longship.'

'No, but it looks like one,' said Faru, as the mystery ship's bow and then its low hull appeared slowly around the bend.

Certainly, this vessel was clinker built in the Viking style with its lowered sail lying furled along its length but, instead of a steering oar, it had a proper rudder and tiller being worked by a rather weather-beaten character at the stern. Nor did it have any oars, its forward progress being maintained by two young men staggering along the side-decks pushing long poles against the river bed. Jenny watched, fascinated. 'They're punting it along.'

'It's called quanting, Jenny,' corrected Max, glad to impart at least one thing his sister didn't know. 'It's like punting, but the poles are called quants.'

'Well, it looks really hard work.' The boat was close enough now for Jenny to see that the quanting deckhands weren't much older than themselves, wiry, but with broad shoulders. Not surprising, she thought, as they were obviously used to pushing this heavy vessel against wind and tide by strength alone.

'They must be going *somewhere*,' said Faru, 'so why don't we hitch a ride?'

Max frowned. 'Can we trust them?'

'Who knows, but let's see.' Jenny smiled and waved to one of the deckhands who grinned and waved back. 'They seem friendly enough. Let's hail them.'

Faru cupped his hands to his mouth and shouted, 'Ahoy the ship . . . can you take us aboard?'

The skipper at the tiller gave a wave of acknowledgement, yelled some orders to the deckhands to stop quanting, and steered in towards the river bank.

'They'll want to keep the boat moving so they don't lose momentum,' warned Faru, 'so get ready to jump when the beamiest bit's alongside.'

As the side of the boat brushed the river bank they all jumped together, landing in a heap on board.

One of the deckhands ran to help and lifted Jenny effortlessly into the air before setting her down on her feet. She was intrigued to see he had a single earring beneath curly, shoulder-length dark hair and she was sure he gave her a wink as he smiled and warmly greeted them all. 'Welcome aboard our keel. My name is Osbert and that,' he explained, nodding towards his fellow deckhand, 'is Elias.' He then glanced towards the stern where the older figure still stood at the tiller. 'Our master is Gregory.'

Jenny didn't quite know what a "keel" was and now wasn't the time to ask, for already Skipper Gregory was helming them away from the bank and yelling orders to his lads to carry on quanting. Osbert picked up his pole, but not before winking at Jenny again and making her blush.

'Now we're on the move, we ought to thank the skipper and find out where he's actually going,' said Faru, ignoring Jenny's flushed cheeks.

They made their way along the narrow side deck beside the gaping empty hold, towards the stern where Gregory was moving the huge tiller by pushing it with his back. He was a large man with tangled grey hair and tanned wrinkled features, dressed like his crew in smock and leggings. After giving the children an appraising look, he asked, 'So, where are you wantin' to go on my keel?' A hard man, thought Jenny, with a voice to match.

'Somewhere we can buy food.' Realising this sounded very vague, she quickly asked, 'So, where are *you* going?'

'South Walsham, to collect a load a peat.'

'How far away is that?' Jenny didn't want her and the boys to end up miles from *Eldridge*.

'Four furlong hence.' The skipper pointed ahead. 'Just around the next bend in the river.'

Jenny wasn't sure how long a furlong was, but seemed to think it was much less than a mile, so they would still be within easy walking distance.

'If we're nearly at South Walsham, Jen, we must be on the River Bure,' whispered Max at her side.

'You're right, but I'm worried that we won't find anywhere to buy food when we get there because, if you remember, the moorings are miles away from the village.'

'Yeah, that's a pain, but it's too late to jump off now. We'll just have to stay on board at least until we arrive at the peat place.'

Skipper Gregory, though, had other concerns. 'So, how will you be payin' for this passage I'm a givin' yer?'

'Pay?' Jenny had assumed this lift would be free. Besides, she didn't feel like handing over one of their valuable gold coins to this grumpy skipper. 'We were hoping you'd just help us for nothing.'

'I have little wealth meself, girl, to go givin' favours,' replied the skipper with a grunt. 'I've a crew to feed an' if you can't pay, then you must work yer passage.' He nodded to the boys. 'Are they yer friends?'

'One is and the other's my brother.'

'Either way, they look man enough to work a quant each, and there's a pile of dirty clothes in the cabin that *you* can wash.'

With little option, they set about their tasks, Osbert and Elias giving the boys a quick introduction into the tricks of quanting and Jenny, in the small forward cabin, scrubbing a few dirty garments in fresh river water before hanging them out to dry.

Back on deck, she admired how well the boys were coping with their new labour. Although the keel was empty of cargo, she was amazed that the two lads could actually make it move. She went to join Faru who was just lowering his quant into the riverbed at the bow, placing the knob at the top into his shoulder and then pushing the long pole sternwards, leaning forward as he walked slowly back along the deck. Jenny followed him. 'You're doing a great job, Faru.'

Once at the stern, Faru gave the quant a twist to release it from the mud before heaving it out of the water and back to the bows for another stretch. 'In Bangladesh, they have to manhandle lots of large vessels through narrow sections of the delta, and I did my share of that. It's quite fun actually, and very good exercise.'

Jenny took his word for that, though, on the other side, her brother didn't seem quite so enthusiastic. She went across to join him. 'Never mind, Max, we're almost there now.'

Sure enough, ahead of the bow and through the

thinning mist, a clearing on the starboard side could be seen, its length stacked high with what Jenny assumed was peat waiting to be loaded. A shout from the skipper for the boys to stop quanting was followed by orders to the deckhands to throw ropes to the men on the bank, and soon the keel was tied alongside. In the brief lull that followed, Jenny stole the chance for a word with Osbert. 'Have you got to load all that peat into the hold now?'

He nodded, wearily. 'Yeah, several thousand turves of it, but the diggers also 'elp.'

'How long will that take?'

'Until late afternoon, and then we sail again through the night for Norwich Cathedral, where it'll be used for heatin'.'

'But, that's much too far for us to go for food, Osbert. Isn't there somewhere closer we could drop off?'

The deckhand scratched his head. 'We will be passin' Saint Benet's.'

The name immediately meant something to Jenny. 'You mean the old abbey?'

Osbert nodded. 'Tha's it. It's a Benedictine monastery and one of the biggest in the country . . . and the richest.'

'That's not far from here, is it?'

'No, just around that bend in the river.'

'Hmm.' Jenny returned to Max and Faru. 'After they've loaded this peat, they're going to be passing Saint Benet's Abbey. The monks are bound to give us some food.'

Max frowned, remembering the time they'd stopped there on a previous holiday. 'But, it's only empty remains.'

'It was when *we* saw it, but remember we're in the year 1209 now, and so it's still a working monastery. The keel will be passing it on the way to Norwich, so how about we see if Gregory can drop us off there and beg a night's food and shelter while the batteries charge.'

Faru agreed, though with some reservations. 'Assuming the skipper's happy to take us, that is.'

'I'm sure he will be. Come on. We can at least ask.'

*   *   *

'Well, thank goodness we've got a lift to the abbey,' said a relieved Jenny after their brief chat with skipper Gregory, 'but it's a pain having to hang about here until he's ready to leave at the end of the day.'

'Especially as we're so hungry.' As usual, food was uppermost in Max's mind.

'Too true,' agreed Faru, 'but at least we're safe staying here with these men while the batteries are charging up and, hopefully, we should get a good meal at the abbey later on. Anyway, with so much activity going on around us, the time will fly by.'

The three were ashore now, standing on the bank that separated the keel from the extensive peat diggings in front of them, just visible through the clearing mist.

'You're right, and Saint Benet's is only about a mile downriver,' said Jenny, sitting herself down on the trunk of a fallen tree, 'so, it won't take long to get there, once we leave here.'

'Easy for you to say,' grumbled Max, sitting down beside her. 'Faru and me are going to have to work our passage again . . . and the boat's going to be a lot heavier with a full load of peat in the hold.' He gave an exaggerated sigh of exhaustion. 'You try quanting, Jen. My back's killing me.'

'Oh, don't be such a wimp,' she teased, grinning. 'You did very well before. Compared to what these poor chaps are doing, it'll be an absolute doddle.' She was pointing to the four scantily clad workers slaving away with crude wedge-shaped wooden shovels, three metres down in a small square pit of waterlogged marsh. It was one of many, dividing up an area about the size of a football pitch.

'But why are they doing it?' queried Faru. 'It seems a lot of effort for some soggy lumps of peat.'

'I know, but when it's dried out it makes good fuel for heating and cooking.'

'Why don't they just burn logs?'

'Because they've cleared so many trees, there's not much spare wood anymore. And just think, if they hadn't needed to dig out so much peat, we wouldn't have any broads.'

'How come?'

'Because, in two-hundred years from now the sea-level will rise and flood these pits to form the lakes we call broads.'

'They look pretty flooded now,' observed Max, pulling a face. 'Those poor blokes are already working up to their ankles in water.'

Sure enough, two of the men, wet and filthy, the top of their heads below the surrounding ground, were digging into peat covered in ink-like slime, while their two workmates threw shovelfuls of that same liquid into the empty adjacent pit.

'I suppose, as the pits get deeper they start filling with water, which has to be continuously bailed out into the one they dug out before,' reasoned Faru. 'But what a back-breaking way to do it.'

That work, however, suddenly ceased at the sound of a shout from one of the overseers and the men climbed wearily up their crude ladder and out of the pit.

'Time for their tea-break?' suggested Max, but Jenny shook her head.

'I don't think so.' She was glancing towards the pile of peat close by the keel, and the wooden gangplank that Elias was securing to the vessel's deck. 'My guess is that they're going to start loading.'

'Another back-buster.' Max rolled his eyes. 'I only hope Gregory doesn't rope us in to help with that too. I bet these poor peasants don't get paid very well either.'

'Hardly anything,' confirmed Jenny. 'I had a chat with Osbert about it.'

'Ah well, wonderful Osbert should know,' said Max, smirking and winking to Faru.

'Just what do you mean by that?'

'Only that you certainly seem to have found a friend there.'

'And why not?' Feeling her face colouring up, Jenny said, crossly, 'Well, do you want to hear what he said, or don't you?'

'OK, go on then,' her twin replied, wiping the grin off his face.

'Well, it seems that virtually all of these peat diggings are owned by Saint Benet's Abbey. They also own other nearby estates that they lease out to tenants. Osbert said that one of the conditions of the lease is that the tenant sends some of his men to work in the pits for twenty-three days each year.'

'Blimey! So, all of this hard graft is provided free and it's the abbey that gets all the money from selling the peat,' said Max. 'It must be very rich. I bet the monks make sure *they're* all right.'

'Probably, but I'm certain they help people in need and do lots of good work too.'

Max shrugged his shoulders, unimpressed. 'Meanwhile, these poor devils sweat their guts out.' He glanced back briefly towards the keel, where two peat-diggers struggled up the gangplank shouldering heavy loads of peat while, on the sidedecks, Osbert and Elias directed the other two men stowing it down in the hold.

'What a dirty, horrible . . .' but Jenny was stopped mid-sentence by a sudden cry from the keel. They turned to see three men staring down into the vessel's open void. One figure, though, was missing.

'Where's Osbert?' cried Jenny, leaping to her feet. 'He must have fallen into the hold.'

*   *   *

A quick run to the keel confirmed Jenny's worst fears for, peering down, she could see, lying prostrate on the hold's hard boards, the groaning figure of the deckhand. The two men who had been stacking the peat up front were standing over him, looking shocked as Elias climbed down from the deck to join them. Unthinkingly, Jenny followed and soon the two were kneeling beside Osbert's motionless body. 'What happened?' she asked.

Elias shook his head. 'It 'appened so quickly. While I was turnin' to check one of the riggin' blocks, he must have lost his footin'. The next thing I knew, he was lyin' in the bottom of the 'old.'

There came a groan from the casualty.

'At least he's still alive.' Jenny put her hand on his furrowed brow. 'Where does it hurt, Osbert?'

But, instead of an answer, he merely turned his head fractionally from side to side.

'Try and keep still.' Jenny frowned and whispered to Elias, 'I can't see any blood, but he looks badly hurt.'

'What can we do? Do you know 'ow to treat such an injury?'

Jenny shook her head. 'No, but I do know we have to be careful in case he's hit his head or injured his back. We need something to lay him on before he's moved.' She shouted up to Max and Faru, whose concerned faces were peering down at her. 'Can you two find something we can use as a stretcher?'

It wasn't long before Osbert was strapped to a wooden board and being lifted carefully up onto the keel's deck.

'Don't like the look of 'im,' declared Gregory when he arrived on the scene. 'No good to me like that, he ain't.' He scratched his head and glanced eastwards. 'The monks at the abbey care for the sick. We could leave 'im there when we drop you off . . .' he nodded towards the pile of peat still on the bank, '. . . once that lot's been loaded.'

'But that'll take much too long,' pleaded Jenny. 'We need to leave right away, or Osbert may die before we get there.'

The skipper wasn't used to being told what to do, especially by a young slip of a girl and, scowling his disapproval, turned his back on Jenny and began to walk away. It was Elias who now spoke up, stopping Gregory in his tracks. 'Master, she is right. We could take what we 'ave loaded now, give Osbert into the care of Saint Benet's, and then drop off this small cargo at Thurne village before returnin' 'ere to load for the Cathedral.'

'We *could* do except . . .' the skipper waved a frustrated hand at poor Osbert, '. . . we are now short-'anded by one . . .' He turned back to Jenny, '. . .unless your brother and friend remain as crew.'

'They've already said they'll do that.'

'Yes, but only to Saint Benet's. Now they must 'elp work the keel to Thurne, where I will 'ave to sign on another deckhand to work with Elias. You must stay with Osbert at the abbey until we return.'

For a second, Jenny hesitated at the thought of being at Saint Benet's alone, but one look into Osbert's pleading eyes was enough to convince her that she couldn't leave him. She nodded her approval and the boys gamely agreed to stay on the keel.

With a grunt, the skipper turned to Elias. 'Get these workers ashore and prepare to cast off.' He nodded towards the boys. 'And set these two about their tasks.'

Jenny returned to her patient. 'Take it easy, Osbert. You'll soon be well looked after.'

Chapter Ten

'Well there it is, Max. Wow, doesn't it look amazing?'

Up in the keel's bow, just ahead of the cabin, Jenny stood fascinated as the magnificent buildings of the abbey rose above the blanket of mist still lingering over the surrounding marshes.

'It's like an island floating on a magic cloud,' said Max, in wonder.

'That's because it *is* on an island – well, sort of – surrounded by marshes. It's a good place for a monastery.'

Max nodded, before glancing around to the stern of the boat. He was feeling slightly guilty at not helping Faru, but his friend looked totally happy and at ease manning the tiller, closely watched by Gregory. Much to the boys' relief, a whisper of wind from the south-west meant they'd been able to stow away their quants and, with much straining and heaving, help Elias hoist the heavy black sail.

It wasn't far to the abbey, and they were soon on the final reach. Jenny was kneeling beside Osbert and encouraging him to take just a sip of water, when Max joined her. 'How's the patient?' he enquired.

'Barely conscious, I'm afraid. Thank goodness we're nearly there.'

Max took a good look at the abbey again. 'It looks so different, doesn't it, Jen? When we came before, there was only a ruined gatehouse with the remains of an old windmill inside it. Now there's a wall around the whole place, no mill, and even the gatehouse isn't the same.'

'That's because the mill wasn't built until the eighteenth century,' explained Jenny, 'and I guess this gatehouse must be the original one. It all looks very grand now though.'

Very soon the keel was gliding by flint buildings, some of them two-storeys high, standing close to the river's edge and forming a part of the abbey wall. Ahead was a rather longer warehouse-like building, close to the stone quay to which they were obviously going to moor. From the stern came a shouted order from Gregory. Max jumped to it. 'I guess it's time to drop the sail.'

Jenny watched her brother run to the mast with something approaching admiration. Much as she wished they'd never become involved in this time-travelling adventure, she had to admit that the effect on Max had been only for the good. In fact, she couldn't remember the last time he'd even mentioned his iPad.

And even Faru, whom she'd always thought of as being a swat and even a bit nerdy, had shown himself to be so brave and practical. She watched him now, putting his back into that huge tiller to bring the keel's bow just a few degrees to port. More orders from Gregory, and the halyard was let go and, with a rattle of blocks and the crack of flapping canvas, the sail came sliding down the mast and the boat edged towards the stone quay where figures stood ready to catch their lines. And then they were alongside with just the gentlest kiss of wood on stone, lines were made fast and the skipper was actually smiling.

'Well done, lad,' she heard Gregory say, 'you'll make a fine seaman.' At the same time she noticed a black-cowled figure coming aboard to talk to the skipper.

Jenny remained at Osbert's side. 'We're at the abbey now. I'm sure the monks here will put you right.'

Indeed the one who had already boarded was now beside her, pushing back his cowl and examining the casualty with a practised eye. He was a small man, probably thin beneath his black habit, and old enough for the short-cut wisps of hair surrounding his shaved tonsure to be speckled with grey. His voice though was soft and calm. 'What ails him?'

'He fell into the hold. I think he struck his head and knocked himself out. He hasn't spoken since.'

'Then we must get him ashore.' The monk held out his hand. 'I am Brother Bryce, the infirmarian.'

Without delay, he called instructions to some ogling figures on the quay and soon they were returning at a run, bearing a crude stretcher onto which they trans-ferred the groaning Osbert. And then, by strong arms and guidance from Brother Bryce, he was being lifted up and onto the quayside. 'Take him straight to the infirmary . . . and carefully,' he ordered, and Osbert was speedily borne away through the quayside building and into the sanctum of the abbey grounds.

Much as she wished to go with him, Jenny held back. Unsure of how long it would be before she saw her brother and Faru again, she wanted to say her goodbyes.

'Take care, both of you, and get back here as soon as you can.'

'I don't like leaving you here alone. Are you sure you'll be all right?' Max asked, showing unaccustomed brotherly concern. Jenny's eyes welled up, but she nodded bravely as he put a hand on her shoulder. 'Gregory reckons we'll be back sometime tomorrow, so just keep out of trouble until then.'

Pulling herself together, she gave the boys a weak smile and assured them she'd be well looked after in such a holy place. 'I'll be fine, but I'll miss you,' she shouted, raising her voice above Gregory's barked orders to cast off. In all too short a time, the keel was gliding away from the quay as its sail caught the breeze and the little chuckle of water from its bow widened outwards. Jenny watched until the vessel had disappeared from sight around the bend downriver and then, feeling suddenly alone, turned to make her way into the abbey. But, before she had gone far, a much younger monk appeared on the quayside, his fresh face beaming a smile that immediately cheered her up.

'Welcome to the Abbey of Saint Benet's at Holme. I am Brother Tristan, assistant to Brother Bryce the infirmarian.'

'And I'm Jenny.' She found herself immediately reassured by this personable monk who seemed far too outgoing to have committed himself to a life of religious devotion. 'I am a friend of Osbert, the injured deckhand we just brought to you. Will it be all right to spend the night here so I can keep an eye on him?'

Brother Tristan smiled. 'Of course, sister. It is part of the rule of Saint Benedict that all strangers are received as Christ and given hospitality. Normally, both you and the injured lad would be housed in Saint James's.'

'Saint James's?'

'Yes, the hospital built just over fifty years ago for the elderly, the sick and infirm, and for guests such as yourself. It lies just along the causeway from here on the way to Horning, but sadly we cannot take either of you there at present.'

'Oh dear. Why not?'

'Because there is an outbreak of sickness within, which we fear might spread to the abbey. So you both must stay here for the present. But have no fear, your friend will be well cared for in the infirmary and you will be given shelter close by. Come, let me show you.'

Brother Tristan led the way through the quayside buildings into what seemed to be a farmyard, before emerging onto a grassy slope, at the top of which were the church and main part of the abbey. To Jenny, the buildings were all the more impressive when the monk explained that the stone for their construction had been brought by boat all the way from Normandy in France. Following him into the cool of the cloisters, she listened as he pointed out the monks' dormitories, which he called "dorters", and then the refectory with its enticing aroma of cooking. 'Is this where I'll eat?' asked Jenny, who was feeling the pangs of hunger once more.

But Brother Tristan shook his head. 'No. We brethren lead a very ordered life, sister, at times somewhat at odds with the rest of the world, so we find it best

110

neither we nor guests be disturbed by the comings and goings of each other. So you will eat at the table of our Abbot Ralph.' The brother smiled. 'And, I suspect, better and more plentifully than our simple fayre.'

Jenny could accept that. 'How many monks actually live here?' she asked, fascinated by this glimpse into a world so different from anything she had ever known.

'Eighteen at this time.'

'That's not many. How do so few of you manage to look after such a big place?'

'Ah, but we have something like one hundred and fifty local people working here. They do much of the menial work, leaving us to our study and devotions. We brothers attend eight services a day in church, beginning with Matins in the very early hours and ending with Compline just before bed in the early evening.'

'Wow, that's a lot. I'll definitely give Matins a miss, but would it be OK for me to attend one of the daytime services? I'd love to see your church.'

'We welcome all into God's presence,' said Brother Tristan kindly, 'but first we need to find you a bed for the night. Ah, here comes Brother Dorian, the hostellier, who will do that for you.'

Coming towards them, smiling, was a rotund monk who, after words of welcome, set about showing Jenny where she would be sleeping. 'With Saint James's out of bounds until the sickness passes, we must ask you to suffer our own simple living quarters,' explained Brother Dorian, ushering Jenny into a small cell-like room that contained just a wooden desk, chair and a slatted bed with a straw-filled mattress and some folded blankets on top, 'but at least you will be sheltered and fed during your stay with us.'

'I'll be fine. I'm just grateful for your kind hospitality,' she thanked him, stepping back outside and glancing at the adjacent doors. 'Do you have other guests staying tonight?'

'Just three. We have a pilgrim bound for the Holy Land and on his way to board ship at Yarmouth, Merek, a trader heading north and . . . Jarin.'

Jenny picked up Brother Dorian's slight hesitation before he said the last name. 'Who is Jarin?' she asked.

It was Brother Tristan who answered. 'A traveller, but we know little of where he's from or where he's going. We only know he complains often of abbey life and the dullness of our singing and chanting at devotions.'

'Oh dear.' Jenny was spared any further discussion by the steady clang of a nearby bell.

The young monk's eyebrows rose. 'Ah, the call to High Mass. We must leave you now and attend.'

'Of course, but I'd like to visit Osbert and see if he's recovering,' requested Jenny, as she and the two monks joined other cowled figures making their silent way around the cloisters towards the church entrance. Here, Brothers Tristan and Dorian gave her directions to the infirmary and then departed for their service.

Hoping she would find her friend much improved, Jenny made her way, strangely comforted by the spiritual chanting in Latin coming from the church and echoing around the cloister walls.

Arriving at the infirmary, she was surprised to find the infirmarian still in his dispensary. 'Brother Bryce . . . I thought you would be at the service?'

'When other of The Lord's duties call, we are

112

excused.' He waved his arm towards an inner room. 'I need to stay close to your friend Osbert, until he shows signs of recovery.'

'How is he?'

'Still of another world, I am afraid.' Brother Bryce led her into the small room in which Osbert lay, still barely moving, on a simple bed. 'I have felt his bones and detect nothing broken. The injury must lie solely in his head and for that I have given him infusions of camomile and lemon balm which should ease any pain and calm the spirit.'

Jenny glanced around the sickroom, a dark chamber with no windows, its atmosphere thankfully sweetened by the aroma of the lemon balm. 'It's very dark and airless in here. Wouldn't some fresh air help?'

'I think, for the moment, subdued light will serve him better.' Sensing Jenny's concern, the brother put a reassuring hand on her shoulder. 'Fear not, sister, all will be well. I have just received the good news that the sickness at Saint James's is now under control. We will keep Osbert here for tonight and then transfer him to the hospital tomorrow.' From the other side of the cloisters came the single stroke of the abbey bell. 'Ah, High Mass is ended, and that's the call to midday meal. Brother Tristan will be here shortly so, come, let me escort you to the abbot's lodgings so you can eat too.'

The infirmarian led her back out of the main abbey and down the slope towards the riverside buildings she had seen when first approaching Saint Benet's. Abbot Ralph's lodgings turned out to be a two-storey house-like structure overlooking the river. Brother Bryce told her to wait in the entrance hall while he went into an adjacent room to announce her arrival. He returned almost immediately and beckoned her to follow him into this inner sanctum.

Jenny entered what was clearly the dining room, a large wood-beamed chamber, spartan in its furnishings and with only a crucifix to adorn the walls, beneath which, at the head of a long refectory table, sat the abbot himself.

Abbot Ralph turned out to be a thin, elderly, somewhat stern-looking man. Offering a silent hand in greeting, he then ushered Jenny onto one of the benches at the table where three other men were already seated. She assumed these were her fellow guests. One, clothed in a simple cloak, smiled weakly before avoiding further eye contact, while beside him a loutish unshaven man didn't look up at all. Across from him sat the third guest, younger and better dressed than the other two and seemingly more friendly. Jenny took the bench seat next to him and straightway the abbot intoned a short prayer in Latin. Unable to understand a word, Jenny merely clasped her hands like the others, though she noticed the surly one made no effort whatsoever at religious observance.

Prayers over, the young man beside her turned and smiled. 'You must be the girl from the boat that brought the injured deckhand?'

'That's right. How did you know that?'

'Oh, word soon spreads in Saint Benet's.' He looked concerned. 'How fairs he?'

'Not much better. He's still only semi-conscious.' Before Jenny could explain further, servants entered with trays of food and were soon placing a bowl of what looked like oatmeal containing lumps of meat and vegetable in front of her. So much for the superior "fayre", she thought, but she was hungry and gratefully dug in. After a few mouthfuls, she turned back to her young neighbour. 'You must be Merek, the trader.'

'Quite so and this . . .' he indicated the shy man just finishing his meal, '. . . is Father Brom making his way to the Holy Land and this . . .'

'. . . is Jarin,' said Jenny, having little doubt as to the identity of the oaf now licking his bowl. She turned hastily back to Merek.

'Are you travelling far?'

He nodded. 'Further north to sell the goods I bought yesterday in Yarmouth.'

Across the table, Jarin pushed away his bowl with a snort and beckoned the serving lad. 'Bring me my cheese and ale.'

'A man of simple taste,' commented Merek with a smile to Jenny, but obviously intending to be heard by everyone.

Jarin grabbed the tankard and plate of cheese just served and quickly emptied both. 'Bah. They have plenty enough gold here to feed us lesser mortals better than this.' Pushing away the tankard and plate with a sneer, he stood up and promptly exited the room in a black cloud of discontent.

The trader turned to Abbot Ralph. 'I beg forgiveness, abbot, for such uncouth behaviour.'

'We are not all blessed with manners, Merek.' The abbot closed his eyes momentarily. 'I can only pray that Jarin will one day find peace from whatever has so embittered his soul.'

Jenny though, was more intrigued by something disclosed in Jarin's outburst. She turned back to Merek and asked in lowered voice, 'What did Jarin mean about the gold?'

The trader raised his eyes. 'Ah, the abbey plate . . . gold and other priceless artefacts donated by bene-factors and well-wishers over the years. If you attend the church, you will see it on display. Leofrick will be proud to show you.'

'Leofrick?'

'Brother Leofrick, the sacristan. He cares for all the abbey treasure and possessions . . .' the trader gave a smile and a wink, '. . . but not without worry, judging by the good brother's ever-troubled look. And now I must go and check my own accounts ready for departure tomorrow.' Excuses made, Merek departed, quickly followed by the ever-silent pilgrim.

Left alone with the abbot, Jenny thought that even in this place of peace and tranquillity, there was still strife enough for men to grumble and moan.

*   *   *

After the midday meal, Jenny had chosen to wander through the grounds in the warm sunshine, enjoying the sight of sheep grazing and the well-kept gardens being tended. Beyond these she had seen several rect-angular ponds of varying sizes where two men were using wooden rakes to drag out floating weed. As one of them paused to rest and straighten his back, Jenny had taken the opportunity to ask him the purpose of the ponds, and found they were for breeding pike, to be eaten on special feast days or for important guests. Leaving the men to continue their labours, she had moved on and walked towards the river, clearly the main means of transport to Saint Benet's, and found another small wharf just outside the outer wall by the open abbey gate. Across the narrow channel serving it, lay a small bridge which, she presumed, led to the causeway stretching towards Horning, the village where Brother Tristan said most of the local workers lived.

Jenny would have liked to explore more, but it had been an eventful day and, realising how tired she was, she had returned to her room for a quick nap, only to wake to the steady tolling of the abbey bell calling the brothers to yet more devotions.

For a few seconds, as she rubbed the sleep from her eyes, Jenny had to think where she was and what she was doing. At first she thought the bell must be for late-afternoon Vespers, but a glance through the small window in her cell showed the light almost gone. Goodness, she'd slept the evening away and they were probably calling evening Compline. Remembering her promise to attend at least one service, she jumped off the bed, splashed some cold water on her face from the jug on the table, and hurriedly made her way back along the cloisters to the church entrance.

Inside, the brothers were already in their pews either side of the altar, standing in uniform lines of black, their cowled heads bowed and silent. One though glanced up with a quick smile and she recognised him as Brother Tristan, welcoming as ever, but earning an immediate harsh glare of disapproval from Abbot Ralph. Suppressing a smile of her own, Jenny quietly took a seat in one of the empty pews at the back of the nave.

Seated on the far side was the pilgrim, but there was no sign of the other two guests. By now, the sun was almost set and, with just a few candles and a small incense-burner above the High Altar, the church was in semi-darkness. Clearly the monks knew by heart the Latin creeds echoing off the stone and flint walls.

Unable to follow the service, Jenny studied the church's small but impressive interior where arched mullion windows rose majestically to the high vaulted ceiling, hazy in the incense-laden air.

By now Abbot Ralph had moved away from his position by the High Altar to reveal an ancient table, finely carved, and on it, sparkling in the dim light of the incense lamp, a magnificent display of gold. Jenny couldn't believe her eyes. This must be the abbey treasure which Jarin had moaned about. She was still recalling his words when the service ended, the abbot and monks filed out, and she was left alone. In spite of the eerie silence that filled the building, the sheer beauty of the display drew her closer.

The riches took her breath away: golden crucifixes, altar vessels, ornamental plate, a set of candlesticks and, most striking of all, a chalice, probably used for the sacrament, its glistening form inset with the added sparkle of precious gems. She could understand grumpy Jarin's bitter comments about the abbey's wealth; the value of this chalice alone was probably enough to feed the locals for the rest of their lives.

'You seem to have an absorbing interest in our treasures, sister.'

Startled, Jenny spun around, realising she'd been so engrossed she hadn't heard the sandaled footfall of the monk now fixing her with an accusing stare.

'I . . . I was just thinking how beautiful they are.' She nodded towards the table. 'Particularly that chalice.'

'Yes,' said the monk. 'Legend has it, that it came from a Viking raid, but now it is in the safe keeping of the abbey, together with these other bequests to the order.'

Jenny was studying the sour, anxious-looking face beneath the cowl. 'You must be Brother Leofrick, the sacristan?'

'I bear that wearisome office, yes. I am responsible for the abbey's linen, robes and vestments, as well as its gold and silver.'

'Then I must leave you so you can put them away,' said Jenny, keen to escape from this dismal man.

'They are not put away.'

'But surely they need to be kept somewhere safe?'

'They are kept under lock and key at times,' explained the sacristan, 'but the brothers draw inspiration from their display and, with the services so frequent, it hardly seems worth their removal.'

'But aren't you afraid they'll be stolen?'

'Not in an abbey, my dear. This is sacred ground.'

Returning to her cell, Jenny found she didn't share the Benedictine's simple faith that in a holy place like Saint Benet's, such valuable treasures would be safe from thieves. It was a slightly disturbing thought as she rolled onto her hard bed and went back to sleep.

*   *   *

That sleep seemed all too short before yet another ringing of the bell disturbed her slumbers, this time calling the monks to Matins, the service that was held in the very early hours of the morning. Accepting this as just another aspect of monastery life, but with no intention of attending, she instead lay awake listening to the distant monastic chants until all went quiet and she knew yet another service had ended.

Unfortunately, she found it hard to get back to sleep, her thoughts filled with all she'd seen and heard in the last twenty-four hours and also of Max and Faru's return later in the day. After a while, frustrated with tossing and turning on the straw mattress and thinking some fresh air might help, she got up, slipped on her cloak, and went out into the cloisters.

All here was silent, the monks back in their dormitory and the whole abbey bathed in the light of a beautiful full moon. As Jenny paused to sit on the low cloister wall, gazing up into the cloudless heavens where a myriad of stars shone and twinkled, something caught her eye.

It was just a slight movement in the grass quadrangle, an area surrounded by the four sides of the cloisters. She sat watching, thinking she might have imagined it. Then it moved again, this time outside the shadow of the cloisters, the dark shape of a monk's habit skulking swiftly through the moonlight, feet silent on the soft turf. Perhaps one of the brothers was finding it difficult to sleep too, but why did he look so furtive?

Jenny followed the monk's wraith-like creep until he reached the cloister directly by the church entrance, where he slid over the low wall with surprising dexterity for one living the monastic life. Then she heard the slight creak of the church door opening and the figure vanished.

Somehow, she sensed something was wrong and, for a second, considered sneaking up to the church to see just what was going on. Then she remembered Max's warning to keep out of trouble. This was none of her business, and besides, she was beginning to feel cold. With a little shudder, she pulled her cloak about her and tiptoed silently back to her cell.

Chapter Eleven

Clang . . . clang . . . CLANG!

Once again it was that persistent bell waking Jenny out of what seemed like only a minute's sleep. Then she remembered that the Lauds service followed not long after Matins and once again the monks were being called to prayer.

Except, this time the ringing of the abbey bell was not the usual steady toll, but a continuous peal that seemed to have a sense of urgency behind it. Perhaps the abbey was on fire or something equally calamitous? Once again Jenny pulled on her cloak and went out into the chill morning air.

Immediately, she knew that something was badly wrong. Monks were scurrying along the cloisters towards the church with mutterings and none of their usual gliding calm. She followed them to the church door where several others were already gathered under the withering eye of Abbot Ralph. She noticed the friendly assistant infirmarian amongst them and edged to his side.

'Brother Tristan . . . what's happening?'

'Something terrible. The theft of some of the abbey's treasure.'

'Oh, no! What's been taken?'

'The jewelled communion chalice . . . the most valuable of all our possessions.'

Overhearing this exchange, Abbot Ralph intervened. 'Do you know anything of this, sister?'

Jenny blinked twice. 'No, of course not.'

'A quick denial, sister . . .' It was Brother Leofrick, the dour sacristan, quick to join the little group now surrounding her, '. . . though you were showing uncommon interest in our holy chattels after Compline.'

'Yes, but only to admire them.' Suddenly Jenny felt their condemnation all set to take her in its grip. 'You surely don't think *I* stole it?'

'What are we to think?' The sacristan seemed eager to shift blame away from his own neglect. 'You are a guest here of strange behaviour and a life of which we know nothing. Perhaps you took advantage of our hospitality for the sole purpose of stealing from us. Perhaps . . .'

But Jenny cut him off. 'Stop this. I took nothing, but I did see something . . . last night, sometime after Matins.'

'Saw what, sister?' Abbot Ralph was fixing her with suspicious eyes. 'Speak up, girl.'

'I saw a monk . . . scurrying across the grass quadrangle towards the church . . . he seemed . . .'

'A monk!' It was the sacristan again, his voice filled with scorn. 'Are you suggesting that one of our own brothers could commit such a crime?' He turned to the abbot. 'She is making this up to cover her own sin, and should be held and the sheriff summoned.'

'She is not the one you seek.' Jenny swung around, to see Brother Dorian, the jovial hostellier, walking towards them. 'I have just checked the other guest cells and Jarin has disappeared.'

'Jarin!' The name was repeated by more than one of the brothers, all of whom had probably heard this rough traveller's scorn for religious wealth, but it was Abbot Ralph who turned to Leofrick.

'When could the theft have happened?'

'Anytime after Matins. I came to check the church for Lauds and found the chalice gone.'

'Then, if what our sister saw was Jarin about his evil quest, he is now far away.' The abbot turned to the assembled brothers. 'There is little we can do until daybreak. Return to your dormitory and I will see you at Prime, when we will pray that this sinner will soon be brought to justice and our treasure recovered.'

As the monks dispersed, Jenny returned to her cell. Glad as she was to have suspicion lifted from her own shoulders, she wondered if it really was Jarin she had spotted, sneaking across the quadrangle. He certainly had a motive, but the cowled figure she had seen had seemed much fitter and leaner than the short and stocky traveller. Perhaps the dawn might bring more revelations, but she seriously doubted if these monks were worldly enough to investigate the crime. She went to sleep thinking that perhaps her time before the boys' return might well be spent trying to solve it herself.

*   *   *

Not that she was going to discover anything at breakfast where Abbot Ralph was conspicuous by his absence. Just as well, thought Jenny, sensing the atmosphere of shock and resentment that seemed to have afflicted even the amiable Merek, who was eating silently at the other end of the table, as if suspicion was a disease you could catch. Reminding herself that these were very different times, Jenny didn't try and talk, but ate just one slice of bread and then left for the infirmary to see how poor Osbert was getting on.

At least there was good news here, for she found the deckhand much better, sitting up in bed and just finishing a bowl of oats.

'Osbert, how wonderful.' She sat beside him and took his hand. 'I was afraid you might not recover.'

He smiled and squeezed her hand in return. 'I feel much better now, but I still can't remember what 'appened and 'ow I ended up in 'ere.'

Jenny explained about the accident, but it seemed the whole horrible business had been erased from the deckhand's mind.

'They tell me I 'ave you to thank for my recovery.'

She shook her head. 'I only did what I could. It's the brothers of Saint Benet's that gave you the treatment you needed. To get you well completely, they plan to transfer you to Saint James' hospital later today.'

'Yes, they 'ave been very kind, but I don't think I need the 'ospital now. Better that I get back to the boat and 'elp Elias.'

'If you're really sure you're up to it.' Jenny smiled and stroked his muscular arm. 'With last night's incident, I think they'll be glad to see the back of all us visitors.'

'Why, what 'appened?'

'A theft . . . from the abbey church itself.' She went on to relate the night's events.

'So, is it this Jarin fella who is the culprit?'

'It seems that way, because why would he vanish so suddenly if he's innocent? They've searched the whole abbey, but he's definitely gone, which means he must've escaped along the causeway to Horning.' Jenny sighed. 'He had to be desperate to risk going across the marshes in the dark. It would be so easy to fall into the reedbeds and be sucked down into the mud.'

But Osbert shook his head. 'Not last night, Jenny. With the full moon, it was almost as bright as day. He would 'ave 'ad no problem finding 'is way.'

'I suppose not, but I'm still not convinced he *was* the thief. In fact, I'm going off to the church right now.'

'What, to pray for 'is soul?'

'No,' explained Jenny, giving Osbert a goodbye peck on the cheek. 'I need to check the crime scene for any clues.'

*   *   *

Entering the church, she was pleased to see she had the building to herself though, without the monks at prayer, it felt cold and empty and even the sacred High Altar seemed to have lost some of its mysticism. Jenny turned her attention to the heavy oak table on which the treasure had stood. It was empty now, Brother Leofrick obviously having finally locked the remaining riches away.

Jenny examined the altar carefully, looking for the clue that might point to the identity of the thief. It was only when she was about to leave that something caught her eye, glinting on the ground beneath its heavy oak top. She picked it up, turning it over in her fingers, wishing in some ways she had never found it, but knowing it confirmed her suspicions. Pocketing the find, she left the church and made her way into the abbey grounds, unsure of what she should do next.

Outside, the early morning sky was still clear and blue with just a chill to the slight breeze. Jenny looked downriver, but there was no sign of the keel returning, so she made her way down towards the main gate and the Horning causeway, along which some of the locals were just arriving for work. Further along it, others were moving to the side to let two men on horseback pass. Between them was a stumbling figure being half-dragged on the end of a rope. Soon, this party was entering through the gatehouse where workers and monks alike gathered to witness this unexpected event. Jenny joined them and, as the two horsemen reined to a halt, she saw that the prisoner was the errant Jarin.

He was now a worn and haggard version of the blustering bully they had known, having clearly suffered much rough handling in the last hours. But why had he been arrested, seeing as news of the theft hadn't yet left the abbey? Whatever, Abbot Ralph himself was soon on the scene and beaming with satisfaction.

'Greetings, Sheriff. It is indeed good to see you and your sergeant so promptly. And with the thief of our sacred chalice already in hand. How did you apprehend him so quickly?'

The sheriff looked confused. 'Abbot, I know of no such theft.'

'Then why have you arrested this scoundrel?'

'Because he is a man wanted for murder.'

There came a little gasp from the small crowd surrounding the horsemen. 'Murder?'

'Yes, committed in Norwich not a week ago where this Jarin killed another in a fight over a woman. We have been searching for him since, until word came that he was seeking sanctuary at Saint Benet's. We were riding here to enquire, when we spotted him on the Horning causeway.' He gave the fugitive a hefty kick with his boot. 'And now we come to plead some food and water before taking him back to Norwich for trial.'

'But what of our chalice?' pleaded Abbot Ralph. 'The treasure he stole from the holy church.'

'We found no treasure on this man.'

'Then he must have hidden it before he was captured.' Abbot Ralph sighed. 'We will search for it along the way, but first let me offer you the hospitality of our house of God.'

The sheriff went off, following the abbot to his lodgings and leaving the sergeant to guard both his horse and the luckless Jarin, the latter still the subject of much loud jeering and the odd rotten vegetable thrown by the angry crowd.

Jenny chose to wander the other way. Clearly, Jarin was an evil man and destined to hang, but after viewing the fugitive once more in the flesh, she was more certain than ever he was not the nocturnal figure she had seen on his way to rob the church.

Such disturbing thoughts, however, were soon washed away by the sight of a tall mast and square black sail just rounding the bend before the abbey moorings. Excitedly, she went running towards the quay, arriving as the first lines were being thrown ashore. And there, on deck waving madly, were Max and Faru. Jumping down onto the quay as soon as the ropes were made fast, the boys hugged her as though they'd been apart for years.

'Oh, Jenny, it's great to see you. Has everything been all right?' asked Max.

'It's, um, had its moments,' she admitted.

'Why, what's happened?' Faru had detected the hesitation in her voice.

'Oh gosh, where do I start?' But she did start and managed to briefly fill them in on the abbey theft and its consequences.

At the end, Max shook his head. 'So, what happens now?'

'I'm not sure, but perhaps *this* monk can tell us.'

Brother Tristan, the assistant infirmarian, had just joined them on the quay. 'I'm pleased to tell you, sister, that Osbert is well enough to return to his job and family. Some of our workers are already helping him walk here.'

'Oh, that's wonderful news.' Jenny looked towards Skipper Gregory standing at the keel's stern. 'I'm sure his master will be delighted to have him back.'

By now, the injured deckhand was stumbling onto the quay, supported by two abbey workers, followed by a third holding his few meagre belongings wrapped in a cloth bag. Elias seemed thrilled to welcome his fellow crewman back onboard and was about to carry his bag for him when Jenny leapt in to save him the trouble.

'Here, let *me* take that.' She grabbed the bag, but in her eagerness, managed to drop it. It hit the deck with a surprising clang and burst open. For a few seconds everyone stared at the contents laying exposed for all to see: a leather purse, Osbert's seaman's knife and, most striking of all, a golden chalice encrusted with precious stones.

'You little fool.' It was Osbert's harsh voice breaking the shocked silence.

But Jenny remained surprisingly calm. 'No, Osbert, *you* are the fool, and now you'll be punished for it.'

Soon, the sheriff and sergeant arrived at the quay, quickly followed by the abbot and most of the brothers. Minutes later, Osbert was being marched back down the gangway with none of the care given to him when he boarded. It hurt Jenny to see such hatred in his eyes as he cast her a final look, but her attention was diverted by Abbot Ralph, who took both her hands. 'Sister, we owe you our eternal thanks. Brother Tristan here tells me he is sure you dropped the bag on purpose, knowing what would fall out.'

'Perhaps.' Jenny gave a nervous smile. 'At least now, the abbey has its chalice back.'

'Let's get away while we still 'ave water under us,' ordered Skipper Gregory, shaking his head sadly, while giving the tiller a token heave to each side. 'I've 'ad surprises enough this mornin' without havin' to stem a foul tide.'

More shouted orders, lines thrown back on board, the sail hoisted and they were on their way, Saint

Benet's Abbey and its waving brotherhood soon far behind, as they sailed back up the old course of the Bure towards *Eldridge* and their other life.

Jenny stood watching until the vast religious site and its magnificent buildings had completely disappeared, knowing she would never see them again.

'I think it's your turn to have a bit of heartache, isn't it, Jen?' said Max, joining her at the stern. 'I'm sorry he wasn't the person you thought he was.'

She could only give a silent nod.

*   *   *

'So, Jen, how did you work out that Osbert was the thief?'

They were back on board *Eldridge Echo*, having been dropped ashore by Gregory and Elias, who seemed sad to see them go. Faru had checked the state of the batteries and confirmed they were charged enough for at least a few years travel forward. As electrical circuits came alive and instrument needles went back into the green, both boys were eager to hear her answer.

Jenny shrugged. 'I probably wouldn't have if I hadn't been so sure that it wasn't Jarin I'd seen that night.'

'But, if it was Osbert, where did he get hold of a monk's habit?' asked Max.

'It was a spare one of Brother Bryce's, left hanging in the infirmary.'

Faru paused in checking the instruments. 'So when do you think he planned the theft? I thought he was too badly hurt to move.'

'I think he came up with the idea right back when he suggested dropping us off at Saint Benet's. My guess is that Osbert knew all about the gold left out on display in the church and saw a perfect opportunity to steal it by faking an injury, so he could be put ashore with us. He probably figured that with everyone thinking he was too badly injured to move, he'd be the last to be suspected . . . and he was nearly right. When he heard he was going to be transferred to Saint James' hospital the next day, he knew he had to act that night.'

'He must've thought he'd got away with it when Jarin did a bunk and was blamed. I wonder why that awful man ran away, when he hadn't stolen the chalice?' asked Max.

'Because he knew the abbott would call in the sheriff and, being a wanted man, he had to get away before he was discovered. Unfortunately for him, he ran straight into the lawmen out searching for him on the causeway.'

'He deserves all he gets,' said Faru, 'but you still haven't told us how you knew it was Osbert.'

'It was simple really, because he gave himself away by telling me it was bright moonlight on the night of the robbery. His room in the infirmary had no windows, so he had no way of knowing that unless he'd been outside. But I'd noticed something else and so I went to check the crime scene and found this.' From her pocket, Jenny produced a small shining ring.

'What's that?'

'An earring, just like the one Osbert wore, and it was missing when I last saw him in the infirmary.'

'Well, he won't need it now,' sighed Faru. 'I reckon

they'll give him a hard time, stealing from a holy place.'

Jenny gave a little shudder. 'I'm sure you're right, but at least one good thing came from my night at Saint Benet's, because I now know what I'd like to do when I leave school.'

Max looked horrified. 'Please don't tell me you want to be a nun, Jen.'

She laughed. 'No, of course not. I mean I'd like to be a detective.' Going to the cabin doorway, Jenny sent the earring flying into the river. 'We'll leave that in the century it came from.' Then she glanced at the humming instrument panel, before turning to Faru. 'Now let's try and get some way back to our own.'

Chapter Twelve

'But we've still got almost 250 years to go!' Jenny exclaimed, gloomily.

They had landed yet again and, depressingly, the year gauge told them it was only 1770. She looked through the wheelhouse windows, her eyes adjusting to the almost total darkness. Outside, all she could see was water on which, in the gusting wind, little wavelets formed and collapsed, their white caps barely illuminated by the weak moon beams peering spasmodically between low scudding clouds. 'Oh, what a miserable night.'

Faru tapped the gauge, hoping the figures might be wrong, but they didn't budge. 'Obviously powering ahead in time takes more energy than the batteries can store. It looks like we're in for another day or so of recharging.'

'Another day!' Max shook his head in despair. 'At this rate our parents will have *finished* the holiday by the time we get back.'

'More likely they'll be part of a national police hunt to find us,' said Jenny, dejectedly.

'Maybe, but there's nothing we can do about that except get home to them as soon as possible.' Faru was checking the battery state again. 'A good day's sunshine will help, but if we want a quicker charge, we'll need to start the engine.'

'The weather out there looks horrible,' said Jenny, wiping condensation from the window, 'so let's do that.'

'. . . and have half the locals down here wondering what the racket is,' scoffed Max, quick to quash this idea.

'If there are any.' She peered through the opposite window and this time, instead of open water, was relieved to see the dark silhouette of trees and a distant church tower. 'Thank goodness there's land nearby. I thought we might have come down in the sea!'

'It's probably another broad,' said Faru, 'but I wonder which one?'

'Well, we won't find out by just sitting here feeling sorry for ourselves. The wind seems to be drifting us onto that shore, so why don't we moor *Eldridge* when we get there and look around?'

'What . . . in this filthy weather?' grumbled Max.

'It's better than feeling cold and doing nothing in here.' Faru threw his cloak into a corner of the wheelhouse on top of the others, forming an untidy, rather smelly, heap. 'We won't need these any more, so I say let's chuck them overboard.' With a nod from the others, he rolled them into a tight bundle and tossed them through the open window. 'At least they had oilskins in the late seventeen hundreds, so we'll be able to wear our waterproofs to keep dry.' He stuck his head out of the door. 'Anyway, the rain seems to have stopped now.' It had indeed, and the cloud was breaking up as well, to pour a little moonshine onto the somewhat desolate scene. 'I can't see any sign of life, but there's a windpump over there, next to what looks like some moorings.'

Max joined Faru at the door, staring and scowling at the uninviting scene before him. 'Not a single light or house in sight. That's all we need – stranded in the middle of nowhere again, with no food.' Feeling fed up and miserable, he sat back in the cabin with a face like thunder.

'For goodness' sake, cheer up, Max. We can't give up now, after all we've been through.' Jenny was getting used to her brother's recent mood swings, excused by her mum because of him being at "that difficult age", and turned her back on him.

Ignoring this spat between siblings, Faru was looking for sign of a path, but it was too dark to make anything out. 'I don't suppose either of you brought a torch with you?' he asked, hopefully.

A glimmer of a smile brightened up Max's downcast face as he fumbled amongst his few possessions and proudly held up a pocket flashlight.

By its light, they were soon jumping ashore and tying mooring lines to the stumps of trees, close to the water's edge.

'It's going to be a long walk round to the staithe,' complained Max, extracting a trainer from the soggy ground. 'I reckon the only thing we'll get out of this is muddy feet.'

'Oh, stop being such a grump and come on.' Jenny was already striding along what turned out to be a narrow footpath beside the broad, the torch searching out the deeper puddles. 'At least the walk will warm us up.'

Trudging behind, Max was trying to think where 1770 figured in the history of England. 'If the Naploeonic War's going on, we'll probably get arrested as French spies.'

'That's not for at least thirty years yet,' reassured Jenny. 'Amazingly, I think this is one time when the country's pretty peaceful.'

'That'll make a change,' said Faru, grinning.

Jenny paused to point ahead to the windpump, standing gaunt against the cloudy sky, its sails stilled in a diagonal cross. 'Strange they're not turning in this wind. Perhaps they're broken. Anyway, let's go and have a closer look.'

The path ended at what was clearly a small mooring, but there was no sign of habitation, save the windpump and a small thatched shed close by the water's edge.

'I told you this was in the middle of nowhere.' Max was taking at least some pleasure at being proved right.

'More like the *edge* of nowhere.' Faru was sniffing the air like a bloodhound. 'I'm sure I can smell the sea.'

Jenny agreed. 'And I can hear it too . . . it sounds as if it's rough.' They all strained their eyes towards the sound of crashing waves and, helped by the occasional shaft of moonlight, could just distinguish what looked like the silhouette of low hills on the skyline. 'Do you think they're sand dunes?' she asked. 'If so, where do you think we are?'

'I know exactly where we must be!' exclaimed Max. 'Horsey Mere, Jen, one of our favourite places.' He turned to Faru. 'We moored up here and walked about a mile to the beach and saw lots of seals on the sand. Some of them even swam around us when we went in the sea.'

'You're right, Max, this must be Horsey, but that windpump isn't the one we climbed up. It's in the same place, but it's much smaller.' Jenny shrugged. 'Oh well, at least now we know where the village is. I wonder if the pub's been built yet? You remember, the Nelson's Head where we had chicken nuggets and chips. If it has, perhaps we can get something to eat.'

'Not chicken nuggets and chips, we won't,' sighed Max, longingly.

'Or anything else at this time of night,' said Faru, 'but look, I can definitely see lights over there.' Sure enough, through the darkness, some pinpricks from what might have been lanterns, swayed and dipped beyond the far-off treeline. 'Shall we go and check them out? There's nothing else to do before dawn breaks.'

'What's the point? If we can't get food, I'd rather go back to *Eldridge* and wait 'til it gets light.'

Jenny had had enough of her brother being a wet blanket and suggested that was just what he should do.

Faru agreed. 'Good idea. You go back and keep an eye on the boat.'

'You mean walk all that way back again? By myself?'

'You may not need to walk.' Faru pointed down the narrow dyke to where a small dinghy lay tied to the bank, swaying and tugging in the diminishing gusts.

'What . . . row . . . in this wind?'

'It's calmed down a lot in the last few minutes.'

'But we can't just take someone else's boat without asking them,' warned Jenny. 'That would be stealing.'

'We wouldn't be *keeping* it, Jen,' justified Faru. 'Just borrowing it, and we'll be bringing it back before it's ever missed.'

'And it would be better than having to leg it through the mud all the way back,' conceded Max, warming to the suggestion.

But Jenny still wasn't sure. 'Is it really wise though, Faru? Max really isn't that good a rower.'

'Who says I'm not?' Max never liked being put down, especially by his sister. 'I can out-row you lot any time.'

'OK . . . so prove it then.'

'Right, I will.'

Five minutes and Max was in the dinghy, slipping the oars into their peg-like rowlocks and trying to look confident.

'As you're such a rowing ace,' said Jenny, 'come and pick us up in about an hour when we get back to the staithe. And be careful with that boat. Remember it belongs to someone else.'

'Don't worry, I will.'

'We'll keep your torch and give a couple of flashes when we're back here,' explained Faru, unhitching the mooring lines and throwing them into the boat.

Minutes later, Max was rowing down the dyke and out into the open broad, getting the feel of the rough oars and cold spray on his back as the bow sliced into the waves. He could just make out the diminishing features of his sister and best friend waving from the bank, but he didn't wave back. Sometimes Jenny was just too bossy and Faru a bit too clever for his own good.

A glance over his shoulder showed the vague outline

of *Eldridge* just visible through the blackness. He hoped he wouldn't be stuck on board by himself for too long. Perhaps he shouldn't have been such a pain and walked with the others after all.

*   *   *

Later, in *Eldridge*'s wheelhouse, feeling a bit lonely and, if he admitted it, missing his sister and friend, Max was keeping a keen eye open for any signal from the staithe.

And then he saw it, not the steady flash of a torch as he'd expected, but the spasmodic flicker of a candle-lantern. What did that mean? And then something else caught his eye, on the broad itself - a largish boat showing no lights, its black hull and black sail even darker than the darkness and just the white of a bow-wave to mark its passage towards the staithe. And then another flicker of light from the shore, and it was rounding up and mooring alongside. Max grabbed the professor's binoculars and focussed them on the scene.

The boat, he reckoned, was about ten metres, with just a single mast. The sail had been dropped and furled now, but he could just make out several men loading something into her open hull by the light of that single lantern. There were also horses standing close by. Eventually, the loading seemed finished but, shortly after, another movement caught his eye and he shifted his gaze.

It was the old windpump, still sitting squat and lifeless in the fresh night air. Or was it? Max concentrated on the sails. They were still stationary, but not in the same position as before? He was sure the last time he'd looked, they were diagonal, but now they were like a vertical cross.

This seemed to trigger renewed movement on the staithe, with men suddenly rushing about, lines being cast off and the boat shoved away from the quay. Clear of the mooring, two men were heaving on the halyard and raising the sail. Soon, the black hull was once again cleaving through the broad, tacking backwards and forwards before disappearing the way it had come. Gone also was all light and movement on the staithe.

What had all that been about? Had Jenny and Faru been part of it or, at least seen what was happening? If so, he was keen to hear their story. There was only one way to find out and, feeling it was safe to return, he jumped back into the dinghy and was soon rowing towards the staithe, a much easier task with the still-fresh wind behind him.

Back alongside, he left the boat at the entrance to the dyke and walked to where he'd seen men and horses. It was deserted, but what of his sister and Faru? He'd hoped they would emerge from the shadows to welcome his return, but nothing stirred, save the far sound of breakers and the creak of timber from the windpump.

'Jenny . . . Faru.' No response. He tried again, this time shouting at the top of his voice. 'Jenny! Faru!'

The answering silence sent a shiver down his spine and a feeling of dread at the thought of what might have happened. Where were they? Was their disappearance linked to all that activity at the staithe?

He was still seeking answers when he heard the clatter of approaching horses.

*   *   *

Jenny had watched her brother row away with very mixed feelings and, even as she and Faru made their way along the rough track towards the lights, she kept turning to look back.

'Max can be an absolute pain sometimes, but perhaps we shouldn't have let him row off on his own.'

'He'll be okay, Jen.' Faru gave her a comforting smile. 'He probably needs a bit of time to himself.'

'Yes, but we've gone and broken the rule to stay together, yet again.'

'Don't worry, we won't go far . . . hang on . . .' Faru pulled her to a halt, cupping one ear with his hand, '. . . I can hear voices coming towards us.'

Jenny froze, her senses alert. 'So can I, and the sound of horses' hooves as well.' She grasped Faru's arm. 'Who do you think they are at this time of night?'

'I don't know, but I think we should hide.' He pulled Jenny after him to the side of the track where they crouched behind a hedge, hardly daring to breathe while the mutterings of several men grew ever closer.

Then the first appeared, illuminated briefly in the moonlight, a stocky character in baggy trousers tucked into high leather sea-boots. Beneath a stocking cap, the ruddy, stubbly face was framed in straggling hair and bushy sideburns. Over a striped jumper, he wore an open coat, but it was the two flintlock pistols stuck into the wide leather belt and the vicious-looking cutlass held in his hand that caused Jenny to give a sharp intake of breath. Leading a small horse with two wooden barrels slung across its back, he stopped just metres away.

'Come you on, yer laggards, that wherry'll be here afore long.' Soon, five more villainous characters and half-a-dozen more loaded horses ambled into view. Instinctively shrinking further back into the hedge, Jenny felt a twig beneath her feet snap in protest. The man stiffened. 'What were that?'

The whole party stopped and Jenny clutched Faru, afraid the very thump of her heart would give them away.

'I can't hear nothin'.' It was another in the party. 'Probably some rabbit sneakin' about.' He pulled a cutlass from his belt. 'I could do with a rabbit pie after this. Let me get 'im.'

Jenny closed her eyes, waiting for the cold blade to come slashing into the thicket. Instead, it was the sharp voice of the leader. 'Get back 'ere. We got better things to do than skinnin' rabbits.'

With a grunt of protest, the party moved off again towards the staithe, the coarseness of their language and the jangle of bridles soon fading.

Finally, Jenny felt it safe to let out a deep sigh of relief. 'That was close. What an evil-looking bunch.'

Faru nodded. 'And obviously up to no good. Who do you think they were?'

'Smugglers for sure.' The night air was still chilly, but Jenny was sweating with fear. 'My guess is they've just picked up a load of brandy and tobacco from the beach and now they're off to get rid of it. That nasty one in charge mentioned something about a "wherry" coming.'

'I've read about wherries. Weren't they a sort of sailing cargo boat that used to trade on the Broads?'

'That's right, and they're probably going to load this one to take the smuggled goods inland.'

'Look, I think they're signalling to it now.' Faru was pointing to the distant staithe, where the dim light of a lantern flickered.

'Oh, no!' Jenny clutched Faru's arm again. 'Don't you see what might happen? Max will think it's us calling for pickup and row right into them. We've got to stop him . . . but how?'

'Perhaps we can run back without being seen, and warn him.'

They set off, running quietly, but when they arrived back at the staithe, Faru pulled Jenny to a halt. 'It's no good, Jen. Look, the wherry's already alongside and there are too many men to get past without being spotted.'

They crept closer, the staithe now a hive of activity with barrels and bails being manhandled aboard by the light of a flickering candle-lantern, and the smugglers' crude banter drowning the sound of their own footsteps. The wherry itself was a smaller vessel than Jenny had expected, not much more than an open boat into which two rough-looking crew were directing the loading of the contraband. 'Come on, make it snappy,' jeered one. 'We want'er sample some of yer goods afore we set sail.'

'Well lucky we ain't got the revenue men on our backs . . .' The smuggler glanced up at the sails of the windpump, '. . . yet.'

Eventually the loading was complete, a tarpaulin

pulled over the booty, and the two crew back on shore. 'Right, let's be tryin' some a that brandy.'

A barrel was opened and both crew and smugglers were soon revelling in a drunken stupor by the light of a lantern.

Jenny glanced from lantern to broad. 'I'm still worried Max will see that and think it's his signal to come and pick us up.'

Faru nodded. 'Look, there's no-one on the wherry now so, if we climb on board and Max arrives, we can get him to come alongside and jump in the rowing dinghy before anyone spots us.' From the gang onshore came more raucous laughter as a smuggler fell backwards off the half-empty barrel. Faru took her hand. 'They're too far gone to notice, so let's go for it.'

Keeping in the shadows, they tiptoed towards the wherry and, once on board, were soon burrowing their way beneath the cargo tarpaulin. Here, amongst stowed barrels and piled bails of tobacco, they crawled to the opposite side and peeped out across the broad.

'No sign of Max.' Jenny didn't know whether she was relieved or disappointed.

'Just as well.' Faru looked back towards the staithe. 'Let's hope the party goes on for a while yet and . . . what was that?' A sudden sound had caused him to glance around in the direction of the windpump. 'Jen . . . the sails . . . they've turned.'

Jenny followed his gaze and saw for herself that the sails had indeed rotated forty-five degrees from diagonal to vertical. 'I wonder . . .' she looked across the distant marshes and pointed to where another pump stood out, stark against the night sky, '. . . yes, look Faru, the sails of that one have moved into the same position.'

But windpump sails were not the only things on the move. Instantly, the wild laughter of the smuggling gang had ceased as, alcohol forgotten, they raced towards the wherry.

Horrified, the friends ducked back down beneath the tarpaulin. 'Oh no,' groaned Jenny, 'we're trapped.'

Faru squeezed her hand. 'For the moment, but stay quiet and calm and let's see what happens.'

Certainly, the gang were far too intent on getting the wherry away from the staithe to notice whispers from the two stowaways beneath the tarpaulin. With the thud of cast off ropes hitting the deck and the urgent shouts of smugglers onshore yelling for the wherrymen to hurry, Jenny realised there was no chance for them to escape.

Huddling together, they heard a man staggering along the deck beside them and held their breath as he came to a stop. But it was only to steady himself as he shouted back towards the staithe, 'The sooner you get them 'orses back down the track and out of sight, the better.'

Then came the disconcerting imprint of feet running across the tarpaulin above them, followed by grunts from the two crew as they hoisted the sail. Soon there was the sensation of heeling as it filled with wind, followed by the sound of water sluicing past the hull. 'We're sailing up the broad, but where to then?' murmured Faru, his voice cracking with fear.

'I don't know, but I *do* know it's taking us further away from Max,' sobbed Jenny, burying her head in his shoulder.

*   *   *

Back at the staithe, Max could only stand and listen to the pounding of hooves, and watch dumbfounded as several horses came galloping in his direction. When they arrived, he was relieved to see a dozen uniformed men in white breeches, black leather riding boots and red tunics much adorned in gold braid. They sat high in their saddles, their brass crested helmets reflecting the intermittent moonlight. The leading rider raised a hand, bringing them to a jangling halt right by the water's edge. 'Gone! Damn them.' His voice was refined, but filled with frustration. He swung his horse around and, at the same time, caught sight of Max standing transfixed just to one side. Giving an order to dismount, he handed his horse's reins to the nearest man and came stomping over, spurs jangling on the long curved sabre trailing from his belt.

'Who are you?' He was only young, but Max guessed he was an officer.

'I'm Max . . . Max Watson.'

'Where are you from, Watson?'

'Er . . . off a boat.'

'A boat!' The officer took a step closer. 'Not the boat that landed contraband at Horsey beach just on midnight?'

'Midnight? Contraband?' Max was starting to see what all this was about. 'No, of course not. Our boat . . .' he was about to point out where *Eldridge* lay, unseen at the edge of the broad, before thinking better of it, '. . . is way off, somewhere across the marshes. I came to look for my sister and friend, but they're not here and I think they were taken off in a sailing boat.'

'What sort of boat?' This question came from another official, dressed not as a soldier, but in some sort of naval uniform. He listened intently to Max's vague description before nodding and turning to the officer. 'As I thought . . . a wherry being used to distribute smuggled goods inland.'

'So, what now?'

The naval type looked about him. 'We could go to the pleasure boat and try and catch them there.' He turned back to Max. 'How large was the gang? How many men were on the wherry?'

As Max's confidence started to return, he felt bold enough to throw back questions of his own. 'What are you talking about? Who are you all, anyway?'

'I am Robert Drury of the revenue service and this . . .' he nodded towards the young officer, '. . . is Lieutenant William Moyse of the Fifteenth Light Dragoons.'

'. . . and *you*,' completed the lieutenant, fixing Max with expressionless eyes, 'are under arrest.' He turned and gave a sharp beckoning signal to one of the dragoons. 'Sergeant, secure this boy.'

In an instant, Max knew he was in deep trouble. Already the revenue man was rejoining the troop, still dismounted while their horses chomped at the short grass. Striding across to apprehend him was the sergeant, whose cumbersome uniform, heavy riding boots, spurs and slung sabre, made him ill-equipped for running. With this thought in mind, Max shot a sideways glance at the dinghy, still moored at the end of the dyke. Could he? The sergeant was reaching out to grab his arm when . . . 'Stop!'

Trainers pounding the grassy bank, Max ran for all he was worth, ignoring the clattering pursuit behind him, all his concentration now on reaching that dinghy before being captured. If he could just clear the quay, no dragoon could touch him, but how tight had he tied the mooring line? Would he fumble the knot and be caught in the last second? Behind him came the crash and yelled oaths of the sergeant tripping over his own sabre. Adrenalin pumping, Max pulled the clovehitch off the mooring post and took a flying leap into the dinghy just as a white-gloved hand reached to grab him.

But just the momentum of that leap was enough to carry the small boat far from the bank, while between came an almighty splash as the sergeant, seizing thin air, lost his balance and tumbled into the dyke. It was almost funny until Max saw the lieutenant pull a flintlock pistol from beneath the folds of his tunic. Wiping the smirk off his face, he snatched at the oars and pulled away just as a crack, a streak of flame and a cloud of smoke filled the mooring, and a vicious sliver of wood went flying off the dinghy's gunwale.

This near-miss only served to harden Max's feverish pull at the oars and widen the distance between him and the fist-waving dragoons. More cracks and flashes and splashes of water as shots narrowly missed, and only when was sure he was out of firing range did Max ease his stroke. Where to now?

Back to *Eldridge* was his initial instinct, but was that wise? Starting the engine on his own might be a problem and only alert the dragoons, who could quickly gallop around the edge of the broad. If they captured the boat as well as him, any hope of the three of them returning to their own time would be lost forever.

So instead, remembering there was a way to the main river along what he knew as the Meadow Dyke, he continued up the broad and managed to pick out its entrance in the darkness. He didn't hold out much hope of catching up with the wherry here, but nevertheless, kept his eyes peeled for any sign of a mast standing tall over the reedbeds. Eventually, seeing nothing, feeling ravenously hungry and with aching arms and back, he paused in his rowing to take stock of the situation. He needed to find Jenny and Faru, but where were they? Were they even still alive?

*   *   *

They were, but still hiding under the tarpaulin, worried sick themselves about where Max was, and whether *he* was still alive. And then, beyond that canvas cover came the sound of the sail dropping and oars working. Jenny could guess why.

'The only real way out of this broad is by a waterway called the Meadow Dyke,' she whispered.

'Is it narrow?'

'Yes, very.'

'So, with the wind against them, rowing is the only way they can get down it.'

'Until they reach the main river.' She thought of the sudden panic on the staithe and the speed with which the wherry had got under way. 'Something really spooked them back there. Do you think it was connected to the windpump sails moving?'

'Yes, I'm sure of it. I think lookouts must change the positions of the sails to warn the smugglers that the customs men are coming. As windpumps are dotted about all over the marshes and can be seen from miles away, they're perfect for signalling.'

'So, that's why the smugglers knew they'd been rumbled and why they left so quickly.'

'Yes, and it looks as if they got away with it.'

'Unlike poor Max, who probably rowed straight into them,' sighed Jenny, sadly.

'At least he'll be dealing with the law,' said Faru, 'which is better than being trapped on this boat hiding from drunken law-*breakers*.' As if on cue, the sound of rowing stopped, there was the thump of footsteps around them and the gentle bump of the wherry as it came to a stop. 'We're mooring up.'

'So, perhaps now's our chance to escape.'

But even as Jenny uttered the words, the tarpaulin was thrown back, and standing staring at them was the shocked face of the deckhand. He turned and yelled to the skipper at the helm, before grabbing them both by the scruff of their necks and hauling them bodily out of the hold.

'What d'yer know . . . a pair a spies . . .' There was the stink of brandy still on the skipper's breath as leered over the children, '. . . and we know what to do with spies.'

Struggling to get free, Faru and Jenny gasped as moonlight glinted off the long blade of a deadly-looking knife.

Chapter Thirteen

Max might have remembered the name of the Meadow Dyke, but he'd forgotten just how long it was. He seemed to have been rowing for miles down its long and winding way before it ended and joined a much wider waterway. He was sure that to the left was Potter Heigham, whereas to the right was Hickling Broad and a dead end. Which way would the wherry have gone? Potter Heigham, leading to the rest of the Broads, seemed the most probable, but he remembered the officer and revenue man saying they would try and catch the smugglers at some pleasure boat.

Feeling totally exhausted, Max decided to moor up for a few minutes, have a break, and think things through. On the other side of the waterway lay a grassy bank. Rowing across, he jumped ashore and secured the dinghy to a nearby tree stump. It was then that he noticed the barrels.

They were small wooden casks, about six of them, stacked out of immediate sight behind some bushes. Clean and dry, they couldn't have been there very long. They must have just been dropped by the smugglers, which meant that Jenny and Faru had to have come this way. He turned over one of the casks, found the stopper and dug it out with his knife. With it came a dribble of liquid and the smell of strong spirit. He'd never tasted it, but he guessed it must be brandy.

He was so preoccupied with what he was doing that he didn't hear the approach of footsteps through the undergrowth until they were right behind him. Startled, he spun around, saw who it was and knew the meaning of sheer terror.

*　　*　　*

'Phew!' exclaimed Jenny. 'When I saw that knife, I thought we'd had it.'

'So did I.' Faru shook his head in disbelief. 'And, instead, he only wanted to cut the ropes holding those brandy barrels.'

'Thank goodness . . . but I still thought we were in for a beating when they found us. Instead, they seemed relieved to have extra help rolling the casks up that grassy bank.' Jenny jiggled a bit to try and get more comfortable. 'Why do you think they dropped them off there?'

'All carefully planned, I expect, and it's probably one of their regular pickup places.'

'Which means there'll be a few more stops yet, where we might have a chance to escape?'

'Perhaps, but first we need to think up a plan.' Faru looked about him. After dropping off the barrels, the two of them had been crammed into a small compartment in the wherry's bow, where they listened once more to water flowing past the hull and the creak of its working timbers. Above them was a closed hatch, on top of which they heard something heavy being dropped. 'Oh well, no way we'll ever push that open now.'

Jenny tried to shuffle her position around the foot of the mast which had a large lump of lead attached to it, taking up much of their limited space. 'Whatever's that for?'

'It weighs down the bottom of the mast, making the other end lighter to raise and lower. It's on a pivot, a bit like a seesaw. When the mast's down, it rests on top of the hold and this compartment's empty.'

'So that means every time they have to put the mast up and down, they have to open the hatch above us.' Jenny was thinking fast. 'I know there's a really low bridge at Potter Heigham, so perhaps we'll be able to escape there.'

'Not much chance, I should think. We know too much, so they'll be on their guard to make sure we don't get away and tell the authorities.'

'So does that mean we may *never* be freed?'

'Probably not, but we mustn't give up hope, Jen, and I know Max will be doing everything possible to help us too. He knows we must be in this wherry and he'll be thinking up some clever way to rescue us. Just you wait and see.'

'Let's hope so.' The very thought of her brother brought a lump to Jenny's throat. 'I wonder where *he* is right now.'

*　　*　　*

Closer than she realised, as Max was at the pick-up spot and staring into the face of someone he thought he'd never see again.

'Megan!'

She stood there, holding a storm lantern, its dim light reflecting off the fresh face and long dark hair of a girl he'd last seen seven hundred years before. But, if she was a ghost, she was one that could speak.

'No, not Megan. I am Anna.' She gave him a quizzical look. 'But who are you?'

'I'm Max. Don't you remember me? We met a long . . . quite a while back . . . on the River Yare . . . and, before that, at Burgh Castle where you were called Edith.'

Puzzled, she shook her head. 'I have never been to those places and I have never met you before.' She glanced about them, in case he wasn't alone. 'But what brings you here at this time of night, Max?'

'I could ask you the same, but I think I know the answer.' He looked back to the stack of casks. 'You've come for these, haven't you?'

Beneath a furrowed brow, her eyes narrowed. 'Are you from the revenue?'

'No, but I was nearly captured by them - a whole troop of dragoons and a man from the revenue service.'

'Was his name Drury?'

'That's him . . . Robert Drury . . . I remember now.'

'Hmmm.' She shook her head. 'He's based in Yarmouth and has been trying to catch our gang for years now.'

'*Our* gang. You mean you're part of this whole smuggling business?'

'It's not smuggling, it's *free trading*, At least that's what we calls it hereabouts and where everyone plays their part.' Anna nodded towards the loot and smiled. 'But this being here means the wherry must have got away from Horsey before the dragoons arrived.'

'Yes, but only just, and that's why *I'm* here. I think the smugglers . . . the free traders . . . caught my sister and our friend and took them off in the wherry. I was chasing after them in that dinghy when I stopped here for a break and found the stash.' Max looked into her brown eyes. 'You didn't answer my question. Are you here to collect your share?'

'Not mine, but my father's. He runs the local inn and has to stay put in case the revenue arrive, while I sail my little boat here to collect the brandy.'

'*Sail.* Your boat has a sail?'

'Yes, of course.'

Max took her hand. 'Anna, I must get after that wherry and rescue Jen and Faru. Could you take me?'

She shook her head. 'You will never catch them by boat, Max. They will be far from here by now and heading back to where the wherry is based.'

'Where's that?'

'I cannot tell you until I know you better, but I can see terrible worry in your eyes and know you fear for your sister.' She touched Max gently on his arm. 'Come with me and spend the night at my father's inn and then, in the morning, I will take you overland to where they will be.'

'Will they be safe until then?'

She shrugged. 'Who knows, for the wherry crew are hard men and don't take kindly to spies.'

'Then you're my only hope.' Max made his way towards the boats. 'I'll help you load.' Leaving his borrowed dinghy tied to the bank, he joined Anna, and together they stowed the casks in her stocky little tub with its single mast. After loading, he joined her on board and watched with admiration as she single-handedly hoisted the patched sail and tacked away in the direction of Hickling.

Around the next bend, the wind became fairer and, with the sail set on a steady reach, Anna had time to quiz Max some more.

'Did you hear where Drury and his men were going next?'

'Some boat, but they didn't say the name.'

'Hmm.' She looked puzzled, but concentrated again on her sailing as the waterway widened into Hickling Broad itself.

Churning down its length, Max couldn't help feeling a glow of happiness at being with this girl he felt he'd known for centuries rather than just a few minutes. If only he wasn't so worried for Jen and Faru. They wouldn't know their rescue was in hand.

*   *   *

In fact, they'd had little time to worry about their fate for, soon after setting sail again, they'd been dragged back on deck with Potter Heigham dead ahead, and been forced to row through the low-arched bridge as the two crew lowered the mast. On the other side, the mast's lead balance had swiftly raised it back to the vertical and the prisoners were bundled down again into its cramped compartment.

As the hatch-cover slammed shut, Jenny rubbed her sore hands. 'They didn't waste any time getting under the bridge, did they?'

Faru flexed his aching muscles. 'No, and I can imagine why. Bridges must be the most likely places to be caught.'

'Then let's hope the authorities are waiting for them at the next one.'

That came quite a while later when they were once more dragged back on deck and made to row the heavy vessel through yet another small-arched bridge, again sadly unchallenged by any revenue men.

Back in the mast well, Jenny found it hard to hide her disappointment. 'Oh, Faru, I thought this time we might get rescued.'

'So did I. Did you recognise that bridge?'

'No, but the waterway's very narrow, so I'm pretty sure we've left the main river and are going up a much smaller one called the Ant, which goes through Barton Broad.'

'That's helpful to know. You'll make a great detective, Jen.'

'I hope so, but how about you, Faru? Are you still wanting to be a scientist?'

'Not anymore.' He smiled self-consciously. 'Now I want to be a sailor.'

Jenny looked taken aback. 'That *is* a surprise.'

'Yes, well I've loved handling the different boats

we've been on, so I've made up my mind to make a career of it. If . . . I mean *when* I get home, the first thing I'll do is join the sea cadets. Who knows, Jen, I might end up as captain of a cruise liner.'

'Sounds wonderful, Faru.' She sighed, wistfully. 'Max only wants to design computer games, but I suspect right now his iPad's the last thing on his mind.'

*　　*　　*

Hickling Broad was as big as Max remembered, but Anna's little boat had soon churned its way down the length of it and was approaching a small cut with a few moored boats. Alongside stood a thatched building, not much bigger than a cottage, with dim lights flickering behind small-paned windows.

'Is this your dad's inn, Anna?'

'Yes.' She was allowing the sail to flap now and the boat to slow as they came alongside.

Between the inn and the quay, Max could just make out the name on a sign swinging and creaking in the wind. "PLEASURE BOAT INN." Immediately, he remembered where he'd heard that name before and, without wasting a second, leaned over and gave the tiller a shove, swinging the boat around and causing the sail to fill again. 'Anna . . . we've got to get away . . . quick!'

As they surged back towards the broad and away from the quay, Anna was too busy regaining control of the dinghy to ask him what he was playing at, but once on open water she shouted, 'You fool, Max. You nearly had us over.' She let go of the mainsheet and the sail flapped ineffectively like a flag. 'Have you gone mad?'

'No, I saw your inn sign. Then I remembered what the revenue man had said to the dragoons about going to the "pleasure boat" to catch up with the smugglers. I really thought it *was* a boat, but it must be your dad's inn they were talking about.' Even as he uttered the words, there came the sound of horse's hooves as Robert Drury and his dragoons came galloping into the inn yard. Dismounting, they dispersed, carrying out what was obviously a raid and search. Max allowed himself a smug smile. 'Just a minute too late, chaps.'

'Thanks to you, Max.' Anna looked him in the eyes. 'It was meant to be that we met tonight. You have saved us all, but now you and I must go and hide until we set off to find your sister and friend.' She hauled in the mainsheet and once again her little boat, with its tatty lugsail, was sailing back up the broad before soon turning west into a narrow cut that stretched ahead as far as Max could see.

'Where are we going, Anna?'

'Catfield.' In the shelter of the cut, the wind had disappeared completely and Anna quickly dropped the sail, picked up the oars and started to row. 'There's a small staithe there where we can take cover for the night.'

'Then let me take the oars and you steer.'

They swapped places and Max continued rowing, but it was another quarter of an hour before they arrived at a deserted dead-end where just a few open boats lay moored to a grassy quay.

After securing Anna's boat, they pulled the sail across

as a makeshift tent and settled down to sleep the remainder of the night. The wind had died down now and Max felt a cold dampness in the air that seemed to be creeping into his very bones. Looking east through a gap in the cover, he could detect a slight lightening of the sky. Thankfully, the dawn would soon be here and they could set off on their rescue mission.

Chapter Fourteen

Thoughts of escape were on Faru's mind too. With Jenny sleeping fitfully beside him, he sensed a change in the boat's movement and sounds. Instead of the crack of the flapping sail and the thumps and bangs of the spars against the mast, there came the creak of the oars being worked. He gave her shoulder a gentle shake. 'Jen, wake up. I think they've dropped the sail and now they're rowing again.'

'Umm . . . what? . . . why?'

'I don't know, but perhaps the wind's dropped.'

'Or perhaps they've reached their mooring.' Jenny wiped the sleep from her eyes and sat up. 'If only we could see outside.'

Faru was thinking back. 'Actually, I can't remember them putting anything heavy on the hatch after that last bridge.'

'They were in such a hurry to get clear, they probably forgot.'

'More than likely, but it gives us a chance.' Faru pulled himself to his knees, placed both hands on the hatch and, wary that even the merest creak might alert the smugglers, gave a gentle push. At first there was no movement. Taking a deep breath, he pushed again, harder this time, and was rewarded by the wooden edge lifting just centimetres above the deck. Using his head to take the weight, he peered outside before quickly ducking back down again.

Jenny was anxious for his report. 'What did you see? Come on, tell me.'

'Nothing.'

'Nothing? What do you mean? You must have seen *something*.'

'No, nothing. There's a dawn fog out there, which is why they're having to row. I couldn't even see the river bank.'

'So, no idea where we are?'

'No, but it's given me an idea. Can you swim?'

'Yes, and pretty well too.'

'Then here's my plan.' Faru put a hand on her shoulder. 'As soon as we see land close enough, we'll make our break, jump overboard and swim for it. They're probably far too preoccupied following the course of the river to worry about us and if they do hear a splash, it'll take them ages to turn this boat round and come after us, by which time we'll have disappeared into the fog and hot-footed it to safety.'

'As long as the land's solid ground and not marsh.'

'I'll make sure of that.'

Jenny took a deep breath. 'OK, if you think it'll work, but stay close while we're in the water.'

'I will.' He peered through the hatch for another quick look and in a second was back down. 'There's solid bank close by now, Jen, so I reckon this is our moment.'

'OK, let's go for it. I'm right behind you.'

Faru gave her a thumbs-up before giving the hatch an almighty shove overboard and hearing it splash into the water. Like grease lightning he was through the opening, pausing only to help Jenny up onto the deck, ignoring the angry shouts from behind and the thud of boots running towards them. 'Quick, jump for it.' Grabbing her hand, he leapt overboard, hitting the water as the hull of the wherry went sliding past. Back on the surface, he was thankful to see Jenny close by in the icy water. 'Are you, alright?'

Spluttering, she could only give a brief nod.

'Right, head for the shore.'

With a mixture of strokes, they struggled towards it, Faru glancing behind to see the wherry disappearing into the fog. Soon, they were scrambling onto a grassy bank with an overhanging tree.

For a minute, they both lay exhausted, not even noticing the chill of their soaked clothes as they breathed in the damp air, before Faru struggled to his feet and pulled Jenny to join him. 'Come on, we need to get away from here before they find us.'

They set off along the water's edge, following its curve and brushing past trees that appeared ghostlike in the clinging fog. Finally, Faru stopped and scratched his head. 'Oh no, Jen, I can't believe it.'

'Why, what's the matter?'

'That overhanging tree.'

'What about it?'

'It's the same one we saw when we swam ashore. We've come a complete circle.'

'You mean . . . ?'

'. . . we're on a small island. Look, those are the footsteps we made only a few minutes ago.'

'In other words, we're stranded here.' Jenny, slumped down onto a protruding tree-stump. 'So when the wherry comes back, we'll be sitting ducks.'

*   *   *

Only a few miles away, Max and Anna were preparing to set off on their own search, having surfaced from under their makeshift cover to find the air damp and the surrounding trees almost hidden in fog. Max shivered. 'This is all we want,' he groaned.

'You're right, it is,' was Anna's surprising reply. 'The revenue man and his dragoons will never find us in this.'

'Do you think they'll be looking?'

'Probably not for *you*, but they will for *me*. They will know I was not at the inn and my sailboat was missing, so the sooner we find the wherry, the better. Just keep close to me.'

After carefully concealing the barrels under the sail, they set off on foot, along rough tracks, meeting no-one along the way and creeping through the odd hamlet where only the crow of cockerels stirred the eerie silence. 'So, where to now?'

'Near a village north of here.'

'Is that where the wherry is kept?'

'Yes.'

Already the sun was climbing above the horizon and would soon start burning off the fog. Not long now, thought Max, and it would no longer hide them from pursuing dragoons?

*   *   *

Only a little further west, but still on the island, Faru stared out as the thinning fog revealed a large body of flat-calm water. He shook his head with dismay. 'We're in the middle of a huge broad. Trust me to find the only island on it.'

Jenny managed a brave smile. 'It's not your fault, Faru. At least now we're free and back in the fresh air.'

'Which is getting fresher by the minute.' He was watching the ripples form on the surface of the water. 'There's definitely a breeze getting up and the fog's already clearing. You can see the edges of the broad now and .. .' Words suddenly failed him and he could only point.

Jenny followed his finger and saw the misty outline of a black-hulled boat with its large black sail being hoisted. 'Oh no! It's the smuggler's wherry.'

'And it's heading back here.'

'What can we do? Shall we try and swim to the mainland?'

Faru shook his head. 'No, Jen. You can see the broad's surrounded with boggy reedbeds which we'd never get through. Our only hope is to be picked up by another boat before the wherry reaches us.' He anxiously scanned the broad before pointing excitedly. 'Like that one.'

Sure enough, coming from the south was a small

boat, its sail filled with the morning breeze, a little moustache of foam curling back from the bow and just one person at the helm. Faru frantically waved his arms. 'Hello .. o .. o!'

'Help!' shouted Jenny through cupped hands. 'HELP!' Then she was sure the little boat had altered course slightly. 'Faru, we've been seen . . . but will it reach us in time?'

'I think so. The wherry's got to tack against the wind, but that little boat's got the wind behind it.' Already, the dinghy was close to the island. 'Come on, let's wade out in case it gets stuck in shallow water.'

Step by step, they waded out until they were almost waist deep. 'That's far enough.' Faru waved again as the white-hulled boat kept sailing towards them.

To Jenny, it was the most beautiful craft she had ever seen and it was close enough now for her to make out the skipper. 'He's only a boy, Faru. He looks even younger than us.'

The dinghy continued in and then rounded up right beside them. Faru grabbed the boat's side while Jenny shouted grateful thanks above the noise of the flapping sail.

'You are welcome.' The young lad was nicely spoken with just the hint of a Norfolk accent. Above a thin pale face, his brow was frowning slightly. 'But what are you doing on the island?'

'Escaping from that.' Jenny pointed towards the wherry, now on its new tack and making headway towards them.

'We'll explain later,' urged Faru, 'but we need to get away from here.'

'Right, climb aboard.'

Needing no further encouragement, Faru swung over the gunwale, pulling Jenny after him. 'Let's go.'

Skilfully working the tiller, the lad turned his boat until the wind was filling the sail once more, to send it speeding away across the broad and leaving the heavy, cumbersome wherry far behind with no chance of catching them.

Although the first rays of sun were starting to break through what was now thinning mist, the morning air was still chilled, causing Jenny to give a little shiver.

'Here, take this.' Holding the tiller with his knees, the young skipper shook off his blue pea-jacket and wrapped it around Jenny's shoulders, leaving him in just a white shirt and duck trousers tucked into white socks and buckled leather shoes.

'That's so kind.' Jenny snuggled into the jacket, thankful for its warmth. 'Is this your own boat?'

'Not really.' Beneath his stocking cap and shoulder length fair hair, his features were sharp, but he had large bright eyes and a warm friendly smile. 'It belongs to my sister and her husband and they taught me how to sail here on Barton Broad.' He nodded back over his shoulder. 'My brother-in-law is vicar of Irstead. I'm staying with them during my school holidays, but I live in a village called Burnham Market, about thirty miles away, where my father's also a parson.' He leant forwards and offered his hand. 'I'm Horace.'

'I'm Jenny, and this is Faru.'

'I can't tell you how pleased I am to meet you,' said Faru, shaking the boy's hand, before giving a brief account of how they'd ended up on the island.

'Ah, smugglers.' Sailing backwards and forwards at a safe distance from the wherry, Horace shook his head sadly. 'They are almost a way of life around here. You did right to escape. If they suspected you of being spies for the revenue, I wouldn't have given much hope for your lives. My eldest brother Maurice is in the revenue service, so I know much about their ways.'

'I'm so worried about *my* brother, as we haven't seen him since last night,' explained Jenny, 'and that was at Horsey. I don't know what's happened to him since then.' She paused while they went about onto another reach across the broad. 'Your little boat's very fast, Horace. I don't suppose you'd have time to take us back there?'

The young sailor gave a chuckle. 'She's not *that* fast, Jenny. It would take a day or more to sail to Horsey from here. But I can see you're rightly concerned for your brother's safety.' He glanced over his shoulder to the other side of the broad. 'The quickest way would be for us to moor the boat up, walk to Catfield, borrow another boat and then sail to Horsey from there.'

'How long would that take?'

'Just a few hours.'

They knew it was their only chance and agreed it sounded a great idea. Horace immediately steered towards an almost hidden cut through the reedbeds, and soon they were gliding between weeping willows as he gave orders to lower the sail and for Jenny to jump ashore with the rope.

As they tied up, Faru glanced back towards the broad and, suddenly, his body tensed. 'The wherry, it's seen us and heading this way!' he exclaimed.

'Then we need to move fast.'

At a steady trot, Horace led them away from the mooring and along a rough track, but Jenny, tired through lack of sleep, struggled to keep up. 'It's no good, Horace, I need a break.'

He slowed at the next bend and ushered them beneath the folds of an overhanging tree. 'Just a few minutes. I have a feeling the smugglers aren't far behind us.'

As Jenny took advantage of a brief rest, Faru tried to find out a little more about this kind rescuer who actually seemed to be revelling in the adventure of it all. 'Will you be going back to school soon, Horace?'

He shook his head. 'No, I've just finished with school. In a month I join my uncle's ship, *HMS Raisonnable*, as a midshipman.'

'You mean, you're joining the navy?'

'That's right. His Majesty's Royal Navy.'

Jenny frowned. 'How old are you, Horace?'

'Twelve.'

'Wow!'

But before either of them could delve deeper, Horace put his finger to his mouth. 'Shhh! I can hear footsteps.'

Faru had heard them too. 'You're right . . . and very close.'

*   *   *

With the fog dispersing and the sun rising, Max was also finding the trail long and hard. 'Gosh, Anna, have we much further to go?'

'We're about halfway, but we need to keep moving.'

She looked back anxiously. 'I fear the dragoons will be out looking for us.'

'Revenue men behind and smuggling gangs ahead.' Max shook his head in dismay. 'What a mess.'

'If the dragoons have taken a different track, they may also be ahead of us.' Anna looked worried. 'Men on horseback would find it easy to circle around us.'

'And might be waiting behind those trees to head us off.' Max was studying the track ahead. On the other side of the copse he could hear voices. More than that, he was sure he recognised two of them. Could it really be . . . He moved a little closer and almost whispered, 'Jen? Faru?'

'Max! It's you.' Emerging from the other side, Jenny shrieked with delight before hurling herself towards him, arms outstretched. And then the twins were standing in the track, hugging as though they would never let go, poor Jenny not knowing whether to laugh or cry and ending up doing both. 'I thought I'd never see you again.'

'And I didn't think I'd ever see you again.' Max called over to Anna. 'Come and meet my sister.'

'Anna?' Jenny was sure this rather bedraggled girl was . . . but Max was quick to intervene.

'I know, Jen, I don't understand it either. All I know is that I wouldn't have found you without her. I was sure the smugglers had captured you. How did you escape?'

'It's a long story.' By this time, Faru had joined them and the joyful reunion was complete. 'Faru was wonderful, Max, but we also had help from an outsider.' She beckoned their own rescuer to join them. 'This is Horace who saved our lives.'

The two boys shook hands, but before there could be more words of thanks, the celebration was abruptly broken up by the thudding of running feet. Horace swung around. 'Quick. . . the smugglers. . . they've caught up with us.'

But the warning came just a second too late as the two wherry crew suddenly burst upon them, cutlasses drawn and pistols cocked. Max could only guess that these were the men who had held Faru and Jenny. They were certainly a terrifying-looking pair and the menacing words of the leader filled him with dread.

'So, think you could outsmart us did yer?' His swarthy face was red with exertion and anger. 'Well, yer won't get away again, 'cos this time we'll settle yer once and fer all.'

He raised his mighty cutlass high and all knew that this time there would be no mercy.

* * *

Jenny gripped her brother tightly, her heart agonising in the thought that just as their ordeal seemed to be over, the worst was yet to come. She shut her eyes, waiting for the blow, and instead heard the deckhand's coarse warning.

'Wait! I can 'ear 'em.'

The skipper paused, cutlass still held high. ''ear what?'
''orses.'

The deckhand was right. Suddenly, around the bend, with a clatter of hooves, came a dozen mounted soldiers, bridles jangling, sabres rattling and orders being shouted. Instantly, the smugglers dropped their weapons and took off at a run, back down the track, pursued relentlessly by two galloping dragoons with drawn pistols.

Having spent the night evading the forces of the revenue, Max was certainly glad to see them now, even if Lieutenant Moyse's words were far from reassuring.

'So, a whole bunch of you caught together.' He turned to his sergeant. 'Secure them.'

For Jenny, this was the last straw. 'We're not part of the smuggling gang. We were captured by those two men. . .' she paused at the sound of two loud bangs from further down the track, '. . . who your soldiers have just shot.'

'And who can no longer vouch for *your* story,' completed Moyse with a smirk.

'And we know at least one of you is part of this smuggling network.' It was the revenue man, Robert Drury, now dismounted and staring accusingly at Anna. 'The landlord's daughter from the Pleasure Boat Inn, no less, and who we suspect has long been helping to keep her father well stocked with brandy.'

It was then that Horace stepped forward. 'I can vouch for *all* of these friends of mine, and if you doubt my word, I suggest you consult my brother who is with your Revenue Service.'

'Your brother's name?'

'Maurice Nelson.'

Drury turned towards Lieutenant Moyse and nodded. 'He speaks the truth. Nelson is one of us.' Then he gestured towards Max and the others. 'These youngsters were surely caught up in something beyond their understanding, so let us release them and be thankful the smuggling gang is finished.'

'If that is your decision.' Moyse had clearly been bent on more arrests, but instead settled for having the last word with Anna. 'You are lucky to have such loyal friends, my girl. I suggest you confine your future activities to honest work at the inn.' And then orders were given to remount and the troop left as suddenly as it arrived.

All five youngsters stood breathing gasps of relief, but it was Max who recovered first.

'Phew, I thought we'd had it there, one way or another.' He gave Horace a hearty slap on the back. 'Lucky for us you have the right connections.'

The young sailor shrugged. 'I prefer to think justice prevailed and the innocent spared. But all has ended well, and now you have found each other again, you no longer need my help. Anna here will guide you back and take you to your boat at Horsey.'

'How can we ever thank you?' said Jenny, walking away with him until they were out of earshot of the others. She took his hand. 'And good luck in the navy.'

Horace smiled resignedly. 'Even I am beginning to wonder if I've made the right choice. I want to serve my country and make a name for myself, but England is at peace with the French now and the navy inactive. Perhaps I should have gone into the Revenue Service like my brother. Fighting smuggling gangs seems to be where action and adventure is to be found.'

'You said your brother's name was Maurice Nelson, so yours must be Horace Nelson?'

He gave a sheepish grin. 'Horace is what everyone calls me, but my real name is Horatio.'

'Horatio Nelson?'

'Yes.'

Suddenly it dawned on Jenny, just how great an admiral this young lad would turn out to be. 'Then believe me, Horatio, serving in the navy will *certainly* make you a hero.'

'You think that?'

'I *know* that.' Then she gave him a quick kiss on the cheek and he was gone.

'He was amazing,' said Faru, almost as sorry as Jenny to see him stride off.

'Seemed like it,' agreed Max, 'whoever he was.' Taking Anna's hand, he set off back along the track to Catfield. 'Come on, we've got a few miles to cover yet.'

'And a few years,' added Faru to himself, following on just a little behind the others. He knew the twins wanted to return to their own time as much as he did, but he also knew it meant saying goodbye to very special friends they'd made along the way.

Chapter Fifteen

'Hmm, just as I feared.'

'Why?' Back on board *Eldridge Echo*, Jenny had been relieved to find it untouched and undamaged, but Faru's concern meant they weren't out of the woods just yet. 'What's wrong?'

'Just that it's only been generating on solar panels, so the batteries aren't fully charged.'

'So you mean there still won't be enough power to get us home?'

Faru gave the battery instruments another tap. 'I very much doubt it. It hasn't been very sunny while we've been here.'

'So, do we go or do we wait until they're fully charged?' Max wasn't looking too downhearted at the prospect of hanging about longer if it meant spending more time with Anna.

'Well, if we have enough charge to make it as far as the twentieth century, engine noises will be common, so we'd be able to run *Eldridge*'s without drawing people's attention. A quick recharge, and we could be on our way again, back to our own time.'

'Sounds wonderful,' enthused Jenny.

'I'm not so sure.' Max seemed anything but keen.

'But it'll take ages to fully charge them, Max, and we've said our goodbyes. The quicker we leave and you have other things to think about, the better.'

'Jenny's right,' agreed Faru. 'After all, you've only known Anna for a few hours.'

'I realise that, but I feel I've known her years. . . centuries, actually. . . her or Edith or Megan.' Max shook his head, sadly. 'I'll never forget any of them, but you're probably right; we all belong in our own time and we need to get back there.' He gave Faru a nod. 'OK, mate, do your best and get us out of here.'

As Faru advanced the lever, there came the usual whine and enveloping blue mist, but certainly the feeling of power was less than they'd ever felt before. However, slow as it was, the year gauge was starting to climb and the surrounding marshes were passing below them as they lifted off. Now it was flicking through 1805 and Jenny thought of Horatio and his heroic death that year on *HMS Victory* at the great sea-battle of Trafalgar. A single tear trickled down her cheek as she wished she could have got to know him better. Perhaps she shouldn't have let him join the navy. Perhaps she should have warned him.

Too late for that now though, as she was snapped out of her sad thoughts by the sound of the warning horn and the flashing red light on the instrument panel. 'Battery failure already.' Faru braced himself against the instrument panel. 'Standby for landing. We're settling onto some water.'

There was a splash, the whine of the electrics winding

down to silence and then *Eldridge* was bobbing slightly, the centre of a circle of expanding ripples.

'Safely down at least,' sighed Jenny, 'but where this time?'

'I can tell you that,' said Max, excitedly, peering beyond the wheelhouse windows. 'We've only come as far as Hickling Broad and there's the Pleasure Boat Inn where Anna lives with her father.'

'Not unless she's almost a hundred and fifty years old, Max. Look at the year gauge.'

He did just that and his face fell as he saw the number 1917. 'I should have known, because the inn's changed since I was here with Anna. It's got a slate roof now and it's much bigger.' He glanced around the encircling Broad. 'At least things look reasonably peaceful.'

'Not for the country, it isn't.' Jenny shook her head in dismay. 'We're in the middle of a war with Germany, Max. It's the First World War – one of the bloodiest conflicts ever.'

*   *   *

'Yes, but surely we'll be safe here on the Norfolk Broads,' said Max as they motored in.

'Hopefully, but people everywhere will be on their guard and on the lookout for strangers in case they're German spies.' Jenny was watching the inn and staithe getting ever closer. 'So we mustn't do anything that will arouse people's suspicions.'

'Like what?' Max gave a dismissive shrug. 'We are

British and anyone can see we're not much more than children.'

'Yes, but we look different and people will be curious,' pointed out Faru, easing back the throttle slightly and listening to the diesel's thump settle to a steady rumble. He indicated the ammeters. 'At least the batteries are getting a good charge at last. An hour or so, and we should be able to leave.'

'Nearly home then,' said Jenny, happily.

'Thank goodness,' said Max, feeling more relaxed and looking around. 'It doesn't look too different to life as we know it, except everything just seems very old fashioned.'

'Yes, and the boats are more like the ones we're used to,' said Faru, indicating the only craft lying alongside the staithe, a good sized wooden motor-launch that might at one time have been varnished, but had been painted a rather depressing grey, 'even if it does look like some sort of naval vessel.'

'Surely not on Hickling Broad,' laughed Jenny. 'Why on earth would the navy be here?'

'Haven't a clue,' shrugged Faru. With skilful use of throttle and helm, he was soon bringing *Eldridge* alongside the quay just ahead of the launch, this last burst of backing power causing several men, who had obviously been working on its engine, to stand up and see what this disturbance was all about. They wore naval uniforms of sorts and were wiping grease from their hands onto rags of cotton waste.

'I hope we haven't put our foot in it again,' groaned Jenny. 'That beefy-looking one doesn't look too pleased.'

'And he's coming this way.' Faru threw a spare blanket across to her. 'Quick, cover the computer screens.'

Jenny threw it over the displays before going to the wheelhouse door. She stuck her head out just as the man arrived. 'Good morning.' She looked towards the launch. 'I hope we're not getting in the way of the navy.'

'Royal Naval Air Service, actually, Miss.' He was an imposing figure and, unlike the rest, was dressed in blue uniform trousers, gold-buttoned waistcoat and white shirt with the sleeves rolled up to his elbow. 'But perhaps you'd like to tell me what you're doing here?'

'Oh, just giving the boat a run.'

By this time, the man had been joined by a sailor from the launch who said, shaking his head, 'It's no good, Chief. She seems to have blown a head-gasket. We'll never fix her in time.'

'Great! Just our luck.' The Chief pushed his peaked cap to the back of his head and glanced anxiously towards the south. 'Six-O-Forty-Four's on its way now and no tender to meet it.'

'Six-O-Forty-Four?' repeated Max, intrigued.

'Yeah, a Curtiss H12 flying boat, lad.'

'You mean this is a flying boat base?'

'Not a base, lad, just an emergency landing area in case the sea's too rough at Yarmouth. The H12's a big aircraft and this broad's pretty shallow, so one of our Flight-Lieutenant's bringing her here to see whether she'll land OK.' The Chief gave *Eldridge*'s cabin a tap. 'This your boat, is it?'

'Er, no . . . a friend's.'

'Strange-looking craft. Reliable is she?'

'Most of the time.'

'Get us out to the broad, would she?'

'Yes, of course.'

Even Jenny could see where this conversation was going, and the Chief's next words confirmed it. 'Hmm, well under the Provisions of War Act, I'm afraid I'm going to have to requisition this vessel for emergency use by The Admiralty.'

'You mean you're taking our boat?'

'Only temporarily, Miss.'

'But you don't know anything about *Eldridge*,' Jenny tried to explain. 'It's not like other boats.'

'A boat's a boat, Miss. We might be naval airmen, but we still know about boats.'

'Not diesel engines, you don't.' It was Faru, as concerned as Jenny, but offering a solution. 'Look, we want to help you, but let *us* handle the boat and you just look after the flying bit.'

'How old are you, son?'

'Fourteen next month.'

The Chief closed his eyes for a second and then shrugged. 'Well, not much younger than some of our snotty midshipmen, I guess.' Before he could say anything else, there came the roar of approaching aero engines from the south. 'Blimey, he's here. Right, you lot, prepare to get under way and you . . .' he turned to the sailor beside him, '. . . hop aboard and let's go.'

With the sailor on the cabin roof, the Chief in the wheelhouse, and no mooring lines to let go, Faru backed *Eldridge* straight out, turned her around and headed up the broad. Max turned to his sister. 'Well, at least this is all helping charge the batteries.'

'Yes, but who'd have thought we might actually get to serve in the navy.'

But Max wasn't thinking of that. His eyes were fixed

on an ancient-looking biplane already descending over the broad.

*   *   *

'Wow! Look at that.' Max was watching awestruck as the old aircraft, engines roaring, pulled up from its low run and began a climbing turn for a circle of the broad. 'Do you think he'll land now?'

'Oh yes.' The Chief was watching the flying boat turn downwind. 'Now he knows it's all clear and the water's calm, he'll try for a touchdown. Shouldn't be a problem for a pilot used to landing at South Denes.'

'Is that your base at Yarmouth?' Jenny was finding it hard to believe that this flimsy-looking contraption could actually land safely anywhere, let alone on the open sea.

'Yep, the Naval Air Station.' The Chief nodded towards the aircraft, now on its final approach. 'Here he comes.'

Engines throttled back, the big flying boat continued its descent until just feet from the water, where it levelled off before the tip of its hull kissed the surface, sending a mere feather of spray flying back towards the tail. Then the whole aircraft settled and two plumes of wash went foaming away on either side before it finally slowed right down, halfway along the broad.

'Right, lad,' ordered the Chief to Faru. 'Off you go.'

By now, the flying boat had turned and was taxiing slowly towards them. As they got close, its two engines went to idle, the big four-bladed propellers slowly revolving while ahead of the enclosed cockpit, a figure emerged from the open turret in the nose.

Once again, the Chief turned to Faru. 'Approach it bow-on, son, but take care. She's only wood and fabric and won't take too much bashing.'

Jenny could believe that. Although quite large, even by modern standards, the flying boat, with its biplane wings and complex arrangement of bracing wires and struts, seemed incredibly fragile. Max, however, was seeing it in a completely different light.

'I think it's fabulous, Jen. Flying something like that must be absolutely brilliant.'

'Cold and noisy, I should think.' She turned to the Chief. 'How many crew does it need?'

'Four, normally, but we had to keep the weight down for this trial, so today she's just got the pilot and an air mechanic.'

Max guessed the latter was the figure in the open turret, standing just to one side of two ominous-looking black barrels pointing skywards. 'Are those machine guns?'

'That's right, lad. Lewis guns. Normally, she'd also be carrying bombs, but not today – too heavy.'

By now, Faru was edging them to within metres of the bow, where the mechanic gave a friendly wave and threw across a line. It was caught by the sailor on *Eldridge*, who secured it to the boat.

'Well done, lad,' said the Chief, giving Faru a hearty pat on the back, before leaning out of the wheelhouse to talk to the leather-clad pilot just appearing beside his mechanic. 'Morning, sir. Glad to see you didn't have any problem.'

'None at all.' He nodded towards *Eldridge*. 'Strange craft you've got there, Chief. Where's the tender?'

'Engine problems, sir. I'm hoping your mechanic can have a look at it, but in the meantime, these young'uns have allowed us to use this boat of theirs.'

'Good for them.' By now, all three youngsters had made their way onto the foredeck to get a better view of the Curtiss. The pilot gave them a smile, 'Many thanks, kids. Our Lordships of the Admiralty will be very grateful.'

'Tell them they're more than welcome,' shouted back Max, 'but do you think they'd mind us having a look inside your plane?'

'I shouldn't think so. Swap places with my mechanic, and I'll show you the cockpit.'

Jenny turned to her brother. 'You go, Max. I'll wait here.'

'And I'll need to stay at the wheel if that mechanic is going in to the staithe,' added Faru.

'Fair enough.' With *Eldridge* and flying boat, bow-to-bow, Max was soon exchanging places with the mechanic and then giving Faru and his sister a wave as they motored away.

The pilot held out a gloved hand. 'Welcome aboard Six-O-Forty-Four. Have you been in an aircraft before?'

'No,' answered Max. 'I think my parents are a bit scared of flying.'

'Most people are,' said the pilot. 'It's only fourteen years since the first powered flight by the Wright Brothers, so it's not surprising. Now, follow me, but watch where you're stepping.'

He led Max down through a narrow hatchway

and into the flying boat's cramped cockpit where two uncomfortable-looking seats faced just a half-dozen instruments, the engine throttles and two large control wheels. Ushered into one of the seats, Max breathed in the exciting mix of leather and petrol. 'This is just so amazing. How fast can she go?'

'About sixty knots in normal cruise.' The pilot indicated the wheel and rudder pedals. 'Go ahead and try the feel.'

While Max gingerly moved the wheel and pressed the pedals with his feet, the pilot pointed outside to the moving surfaces on the tail and wings. 'She's a bit heavy to handle, but a good old bus for all that.' Then he glanced beyond the wings to where a gentle breeze was rippling the broad's surface and then up into an almost cloudless sky. 'Fancy a trip?'

'You mean it?' Max couldn't believe what he was hearing.

'Absolutely. I planned to do a few circuits just to get the measure of the place and my mechanic's working on the tender, so let's go and fly.'

While the pilot strapped himself into the other seat, Max cast an elated glance towards the staithe. Goodness knows what Jen and Faru would think when they saw the flying boat getting airborne.

*   *   *

'OK?' asked the pilot, shouting above the roar of the engines.

Max could only give an enthusiastic thumbs-up.

After the exhilaration of take-off with those big engines blasting out their horsepower and the aircraft thumping over the water in a diminishing cloud of spray, he sat in wonder as the pounding suddenly stopped and the broad and Norfolk countryside dropped away beneath them. In a shallow climbing turn, the pilot throttled back slightly and then again as he levelled off. Tapping the altimeter, he turned and grinned. 'See, we're at a thousand feet.' Gazing down, Max was fascinated to see a patchwork quilt of fields, model villages and areas of water that he knew had to be broads. Getting his bearings, he even managed to detect *Eldridge Echo* moored beside the staithe, and the tiny upturned faces of Jen and Faru. He could only imagine what was going through their minds.

And then the engines were throttling back again and the pilot was banking around in a descending turn that had the aircraft lined up once more with the length of the broad. Down and down they glided until Max could pick out the individual ripples, and then they were levelling off before the thump, thump, thump of touchdown, the water feeling as solid as concrete, spray flying on either side, the aircraft quickly slowing and then pitching forward slightly as its own wash caught up.

'What did you think of that then?' asked the pilot as he swung the aircraft around in a wide turn.

'Absolutely fantastic.'

'Want to try another?'

'You bet I would.'

And then they were off again, soon levelling at circuit altitude and the pilot this time indicating Max's set of controls. 'Have a try.'

Max gulped and gingerly fingered the control wheel. Although heavy to move, he was still startled by how the slightest input altered the aircraft's flight.

'You're doing great.' The pilot was smiling. 'Put her into a bank and try a turn.'

Max followed instructions, and the Curtiss was banking over and swinging her nose around the horizon.

'OK, straighten up.'

Rolling the wings back, Max glanced out at their tips to check they really were level. To one side stretched the North Sea, glistening in the morning sun. It was difficult to believe that deep beneath that surface, enemy submarines could be lurking. Up here, everything looked so peaceful, clean and orderly. . . but it was then he saw it.

It was far out, just above the horizon - a dark cigar-shaped image. He squinted to see it more clearly. Was it moving? Difficult to see. Could it be a cloud? No, the sky was clear. Although the pilot seemed busy checking the gauges, Max tapped him on the shoulder and pointed towards the object.

The pilot squinted seawards before his eyes opened wide, he grasped the controls back from Max and instantly turned the flying boat at what seemed an alarmingly high angle of bank, straight out to sea and towards the object. Engines at full power, they went climbing up with Max straining to hear what was being shouted.

Above the increased din, it was difficult to catch every word, but one was sufficient to fill him with a mixture of fear and excitement.

That word was 'Zeppelin'.

It was six thousand feet before they levelled off, the coast well behind them now and the German airship closer and slightly lower.

'He may be spying on our shipping,' yelled the pilot. 'Either that or he's a straggler from a raid trying to get home. Whatever, we need to stop him.'

'You mean you want me to . . .' Max was breathing quickly, and it wasn't only the result of increased altitude.

'That's right. You'll have to man the machine guns.'

'But . . . but, I've never fired a real gun before.'

'Well, now's your chance, because you're the only crew I've got.'

Max took another glance towards the zeppelin. It looked like a monstrous creature from another world, unwieldy and lumbering and now only a short way off. 'We don't seem to be going that much faster.'

'No, but that's why I climbed above it. We'll dive to the attack, but you need to get out into that turret and try the guns.'

Max had no option but to carry out the instructions. Crawling out of the cockpit and through the hatch, he was met by a jaw-aching blast of cold air. The Curtiss might only be going at sixty knots, but that airstream felt like it was from the Arctic. With already-freezing hands, he grasped the twin handles of the Lewis guns, aimed somewhere ahead and pulled the triggers. Nothing. He looked back through the cockpit windows to see the pilot making gestures with his hands. Max thought back to films he'd watched and remembered seeing weapons being cocked. On one side of the guns were levers. He pulled both back, felt a mechanism work, again pulled the triggers and jumped back startled as both guns sent an ear-splitting stream of lead, interspaced with glowing fireballs, arcing out into the clear sky.

Quickly releasing the triggers, he felt the airflow tearing past his frozen ears increasing. They were diving to attack, the bulk of the zeppelin growing bigger by the second. For the first time, Max saw the large German crosses on its side and figures on top swinging weapons in their direction and opening fire. Ominous cracks came from somewhere behind, and he guessed the zeppelin gunners were finding their mark.

Without thinking, Max swung his own guns towards the grey mass filling his vision. As it went flashing past, he squeezed the triggers for a long burst and saw a hail of molten fire shooting out towards it. And then they were banking away as the pilot tore around for another pass.

Had he scored any hits on that first attack? He couldn't tell, because they were already lining up for another, the zeppelin gunners throwing up a field of fire, and tracers flaming past the flying boat's wings. Max had no time to feel scared and once more aimed his guns, squeezed the triggers and fired again. At first they seemed to have no effect, but then he saw flames lighting up the zeppelin's hull.

Once again, the Curtiss was banking away, Max watching with dreadful fascination as those flames slowly became a pulsating orange glow and he realised that he'd hit the target and that the German airship was truly ablaze.

Circling around the zeppelin as it fell seawards, Max suddenly felt the enormity of what he had done and turned away, unable to watch, as figures dropped from the burning envelope and tumbled down to certain death.

Already the Curtiss was straightening up on a heading back to the distant coast with only a widening black stain on the ocean surface to mark the zeppelin's end. Making his way back into the cockpit, still badly shaken, Max paused to glance aft and saw a stream of vapour pouring out of their aircraft's wings.

As he squeezed back into the co-pilot's seat, the pilot turned and gave a grim smile. 'Well done, lad, you did a great job.' He looked rather subdued himself. 'That's war for you – it's them or us, and you have to kill or be killed. Hard though, isn't it, especially when you're only young?' He gave Max a pat on the back.

'You're not kidding, but I think they got us as well. There's something pouring out from the wings back there.'

The pilot quickly glanced up to the fuel gauges. 'Damn, you're right. We're losing petrol.' Suddenly the coastline seemed far away. 'If we can't make it, we'll have to ditch.'

They continued flying in, swapping height for speed against the slight westerly wind. After what seemed an age, Great Yarmouth came in sight and, just north of it, the welcoming expanse of Hickling Broad. As they coasted in, Max was just beginning to relax, excited at the thought of seeing Jenny and Faru, when both engines suddenly spluttered and died leaving only the whistle of slipstream past the flying boat's hull.

'That's it . . . out of juice.' Shoving the control wheel forward to maintain flying speed, the pilot fixed his eyes on the expanse of open water just beyond the nose. 'I wonder . . . brace yourself, Max . . . we might just make it.'

The edge of the broad seemed agonisingly distant and Max prayed silently as they glided lower and lower with fields, then trees, then reedbeds sliding below. The pilot raised the nose slightly to stretch the glide, the flying boat started to shudder as the airspeed bled off and then dropped like a stone as it stalled. An almighty thump, a cascade of flying water, but they were on the broad, the Curtiss running on just a few more metres before skidding to a standstill in silence. Max blinked twice and knew they were still alive. And there was *Eldridge*, powering across the broad to meet them. Perhaps now they really could all go home.

Chapter Sixteen

'So, you reckon there's enough charge to get us right back?'

Having towed in the Curtiss and said their farewells to the Royal Naval Air Service, *Eldridge* and her crew were just ghosting to a stop in a remote corner of the broad.

'I think so, Max.' Faru tapped the ammeter gauges for one last time. 'With all the engine running we've just done, they're finally back to one hundred per cent.'

'Good, and only a little over a hundred years to go, so what are we waiting for?'

Jenny shrugged. 'It's just that we thought you might want to . . . well, hang around a bit longer.'

'Why on earth would I want to do that?'

'Perhaps to receive some medal for bravery. After all, you did shoot down a zeppelin, which must make you some sort of hero.'

'Everyone who fights in a war is a hero,' said Max, 'and there are millions of those in this war. And, anyway, the pilot asked me to keep quiet about my part. Apparently he'd get in a world of trouble with the navy if they found he'd taken me for a joyride.'

'Some joyride,' said Jenny with a grimace. 'But at least it gave you a taste of combat which you've always wanted.'

'Not any more, I don't. War is terrible and the sooner I can forget it, the better. But I tell you one thing I did love, Jen, and that's flying. When I leave school, I want to be a pilot.' He turned back to Faru. 'But the flight I'm looking forward to more than anything right now is the one back to our old lives.' He tapped the power lever. 'So, take it away.'

Faru advanced the lever and, immediately, a healthy whine and the all-enveloping blue mist were all the indication they needed that things looked good. All eyes now were on the year-gauge, already leaving 1917 and advancing through the twenties and early thirties. 'Peace again,' smiled Jenny.

'That's as long as we don't land now,' pointed out Max as 1939 and the early forties flashed by. 'It's World War Two, so keep it going, for goodness' sake.'

'No problem, we're already nearing the end of the Twentieth Century,' reassured Faru. 'Are you happier now, Jen?'

'Sort of.' She wrinkled her nose. 'It's funny. All this time I've wanted nothing more than to get back to our time, but now I'm a bit nervous.'

'Of what?'

'Of what Mum and Dad are going to say. They must be frantic with worry and they'll be so angry we didn't do as we were told.'

'Not to mention how furious the professor'll be with us taking his boat for eighteen hundred years,' frowned Max.

'Well, we'll soon know,' said Faru, easing back the power lever, 'but we must be careful not to overshoot again and end up in the future.' He was pointing to the year-gauge going through 2000 and on to 2010, 2015, 2016 . . . 2017 . . . 2018 . . . it was slowing almost to a halt now, the whine decreasing and the mist clearing, a gentle bump and it stopped. 'Brilliant, we've made it.'

As one, they looked outside to where the old Heron Craft boatyard lay just as it had before: the tumbledown buildings, the dilapidated boats and the big willow tree hanging over one corner of the basin. 'Doesn't it look wonderful,' sighed Max.

'It certainly does,' agreed Jenny, 'but I'm not sure the peace is going to last.' She had noticed the figure of Professor Hazlelade striding back around the marina. 'I bet he thought he'd never see his boat again.'

Another minute and the man himself climbed aboard, a parcel under his arm, and the same smile as when he'd left them. 'Sorry for taking so long, youngsters, but I needed to check it was the right part before the delivery man went.'

All three children looked at each other in utter bewilderment, but it was Jenny who broke the stupefied silence. 'So . . . so, how long were you gone, Professor?'

The scientist glanced at the wheelhouse clock. 'Oh, about fifteen minutes according to that. And, by the way, Mr Dursley asked me to tell you your boat's almost ready.'

'Right, we'd better go then,' said Max, glad to have some excuse for a quick getaway.

'Of course, you'll be keen to start your holiday.' Professor Hazlelade watched them jump onto the quayside and, as they said their thanks and farewells, he gave his boat a tap. 'So, how did you find *Eldridge Echo* in your brief time aboard?'

As in their first meeting, it was Faru who found the words. 'Out of this world, Professor . . . absolutely out of this world.'

*   *   *

Back at the boatyard office, Mr Dursley came out to meet them just as Mr and Mrs Watson drove back into the yard. Both Jenny and Max rushed over and gave their mother a heartfelt hug. 'Oh, Mum, it's so good to see you again.'

Mrs Watson looked quite taken aback. 'My goodness, such affection. And we've only been gone about half an hour.'

'Long enough when you've got nothing to do,' said Mr Watson, giving the children an apologetic smile. 'Sorry, kids, but you know what your mum's like once she gets shopping. I expect you've been bored to death waiting.'

'No, well actually . . .' began Max, before being jabbed in the ribs by Jenny, who promptly added, '. . . we're just a bit hungry, that's all.'

'Yes, I thought it was these you were more glad to see,' laughed their mother, tapping the bag of groceries she was carrying. 'Right, come on, let's get aboard and cook you that promised fry-up. I'm assuming the boat *is* ready now, Mr Dursley?'

'Almost ma'am. Young girl's just finishin' cleanin' up

and then you'll be away.' He led them across the yard to where a rather tatty-looking cruiser lay moored stern-on to the quay. 'Right, here she is. Comfy, but basic.' He turned to the children. 'No WiFi on board, I'm afraid.'

Max's parents cast their son an anxious glance, but his reply was as offhand as it was unexpected. 'Don't worry, I won't be taking my iPad.' Max shrugged his shoulders. 'Far too many things to do without wasting my time on that thing.'

As Mr and Mrs Watson exchanged dumbfounded glances, Mr Dursley tapped on the cabin roof. 'April, you finished in there yet?'

'Yes, Mr Dursley.' A young girl, about the same age as the youngsters, had stuck her head out from the open doorway. She was slim with long dark hair and, with an infectious smile, as she picked up her cleaning things and hopped out onto the rotten quay-heading. 'All set to go.'

Jenny heard her brother's sharp intake of breath. She turned and whispered, 'Max . . . it's . . .'

'But it can't be . . . can it?' he said quietly from behind his hand.

'Go and talk to her, Max, while I go on board with the others.'

So, as Mr Dursley ushered his parents onto the cruiser with Jenny and Faru following, Max hung back with the cleaning girl. 'Hi,' he said, shyly, 'Mr Dursley said your name was April.'

The girl cocked her head slightly to one side. 'Yes that's right.'

'Not Edith . . . or Megan . . . or Anna?'

She studied Max back with some amusement. 'No,

I can assure you it's April, and I hope the boat's clean enough for you.'

'I'm sure it'll be fine. Do you work here every weekend?'

'Only on Saturdays, unfortunately. The pocket money comes in handy, but I'd willingly do it for nothing. I just love being around the yard and my ambition is to own my own boat business when I grow up.'

'Sounds a great idea.' Max looked about him, to make sure his sister and friend were safely on the boat. 'I know it sounds silly, April, but I feel I've known you years. Look, here's my mobile number,' he said, quickly scribbling it on a scrap of paper together with his name. 'Can you give me a call later, then I'll have yours too, and we can keep in touch?'

She glanced at the name and gave a little nod. 'Thanks, Max, I might just do that.'

As Max joined the others on board, the smell of frying eggs and bacon were already drifting from the galley and Mr Dursley was going through the boat's controls with his father and Faru, but Jenny hung back, itching to know how her twin had got on.

'So, who is she?' she said quietly, not wanting to attract her parents' attention.

'You heard . . . April . . . April Landers.'

Jenny turned the name over in her mind before suddenly realising where she'd heard it before. 'But she was the girl we met . . .'

'. . . ten years in the future,' completed Max, barely suppressing his joy. 'So, perhaps, now we know which airline pilot she's going to marry.'

Boat briefing finished, and catching the tail-end of

the twins' whispered conversation, Faru joined them, putting his arms around their shoulders. 'I think, thanks to our adventure, we all know exactly what we want to do when we grow up.'

'And, I know who I'll be doing it with,' muttered Max, quietly to himself.

Fingering the remaining Roman coins in her pocket, Jenny cast a wistful glance across the basin to where *Eldridge Echo* lay, its engine still rumbling at tickover. She nudged the boys as the professor emerged from the wheelhouse, holding something small between his fingers and scratching his head. The three youngsters looked at each other and burst out laughing. 'Oh no, we forgot to take out the pin!'

'Goodness, you've all cheered up,' said Mr Watson as the yard-owner jumped ashore. 'Right, to your stations, everyone, let's get going. Max and Jenny, you haul the stern-lines on board when Mr Dursley casts us off.'

'Aye, aye, Captain.'

Mr Dursley unhitched the lines and handed them across. 'Here you are, young'uns. I hope you have a good holiday.'

'I'm sure we will,' said Jenny, coiling her rope. 'In fact, I think we'll have the time of our lives.'

The End